ALSO BY HELEN SCHULMAN

Lucky Dogs
Come with Me
This Beautiful Life
A Day at the Beach
P.S.
The Revisionist
Out of Time
Not a Free Show: Stories
Wanting a Child (coedited by Jill Bialosky)

FOOLS
FOR
LOVE

FOOLS FOR LOVE

STORIES

HELEN SCHULMAN

ALFRED A. KNOPF · NEW YORK · 2025

A BORZOI BOOK
FIRST HARDCOVER EDITION
PUBLISHED BY ALFRED A. KNOPF 2025

Copyright © 2025 by Helen Schulman

Penguin Random House values and supports copyright. Copyright fuels creativity, encourages diverse voices, promotes free speech, and creates a vibrant culture. Thank you for buying an authorized edition of this book and for complying with copyright laws by not reproducing, scanning, or distributing any part of it in any form without permission. You are supporting writers and allowing Penguin Random House to continue to publish books for every reader. Please note that no part of this book may be used or reproduced in any manner for the purpose of training artificial intelligence technologies or systems.

Published by Alfred A. Knopf, a division of Penguin Random House LLC, 1745 Broadway, New York, NY 10019.

Knopf, Borzoi Books, and the colophon are registered trademarks of Penguin Random House LLC.

Portions of this work originally appeared in the following publications: "The Revisionist" in *The Paris Review;* "The Memoirs of Lucien H." in *Story;* "My Best Friend" and "In a Better Place" in *Ploughshares;* "P.S." in *GQ;* "The Interview" and "Parents' Night" in *Tin House;* "The Shabbos Goy" in *The Kenyon Review Online;* and "I Am Seventy-Five" in *A Public Space.*

Grateful acknowledgment is made to HarperCollins Publishers for permission to reprint an excerpt from "St. Francis and the Sow" from *Three Books* by Galway Kinnell. Copyright © 1993, 2002 by Galway Kinnell. *Body Rags* copyright © 1965, 1966, 1967 by Galway Kinnell. *Mortal Acts, Mortal Words* copyright © 1980 by Galway Kinnell. *The Past* copyright © 1985 by Galway Kinnell. Used by permission of HarperCollins Publishers.

LIBRARY OF CONGRESS CATALOGING-IN-PUBLICATION DATA
Names: Schulman, Helen, author.
Title: Fools for love : stories / Helen Schulman.
Other titles: Fools for love (Compilation).
Description: First edition. | New York : Alfred A. Knopf, 2025.
Identifiers: LCCN 2024037471 | ISBN 9780593536254 (hardcover) | ISBN 9780593536261 (ebook)
Subjects: LCGFT: Short stories.
Classification: LCC PS3569.C5385 F66 2025 | DDC 813/.54—dc23/eng/20240816
LC record available at https://lccn.loc.gov/2024037471

penguinrandomhouse.com | aaknopf.com

Printed in the United States of America
10 9 8 7 6 5 4 3 2 1

The authorized representative in the EU for product safety and compliance is Penguin Random House Ireland, Morrison Chambers, 32 Nassau Street, Dublin D02 YH68, Ireland, https://eu-contact.penguin.ie.

For the excellent Jennifer Barth

God only knows what I'd be without you.

BRIAN WILSON/TONY ASHER

CONTENTS

FOOLS FOR LOVE **3**

THE REVISIONIST **25**

THE MEMOIRS OF LUCIEN H. **46**

PARENTS' NIGHT **61**

MY BEST FRIEND **66**

P.S. **90**

THE INTERVIEW **108**

THE SHABBOS GOY **130**

I AM SEVENTY-FIVE **149**

IN A BETTER PLACE **172**

ACKNOWLEDGMENTS **189**

FOOLS
FOR
LOVE

FOOLS
FOR
LOVE

Many moons ago, my beloved husband, Miguel Herrera—have you heard of him?—gave an earthshaking performance in an event space in the East Village, Henderson Square (actually our friend Hattie Henderson's studio apartment), which completely changed our lives. It was on a warm spring evening, impossibly verdant considering the urban grit, or maybe it was just youth (mine) aromatizing the air. But there was an anticipatory excitement I felt a lot back then, in my fingertips and in my belly, as I walked up Saint Mark's to the theater, my senses heightened. I could smell the dirt at the base of the scraggly sidewalk trees, the animal and human urine perfuming their roots, and the peppery green of their unfurling leaves. Even the weed the punks from Scarsdale were smoking as they camped outside Hattie's building was nothing like the skunky stuff we have now. It was the scent of "something coming," like those old Sondheim lyrics from *West Side Story,* so stimulating I almost couldn't bear it. What can I say? I was twenty-two, finally free of my parents, madly in love, and ready to eat the world.

Hattie lived on the top floor of a five-story walk-up. I'd gotten off late from work and was rushing, so I took the stairs two steps at a time in my Doc Martens and a chiffon thrift-shop dress so flowy I carried a cloud of the stoners' exhales with me as I climbed. When I arrived at the open door, I was breathless and already a little high. The room was full. I could see the stage over the heads of the people sitting on the floor and on folding chairs, and through a crowd of standing-room-onlys. I would end up watching the whole event perched in an open window frame at the back of the room next to the fire escape, half in, half out, but I didn't care. I could smoke cigarettes there, and I was delighted Miguel and his crew had such a good audience. In that moment, maybe for the first and last time in my life, I knew I was exactly where I should be: on the top floor of a tenement near Avenue A, in this magical little bird's nest of creativity, married to a brilliant, handsome man who was crazy about me.

I still believe all this to be true.

In those days, Hattie slept on an ad hoc Murphy bed, just a metal frame with springs that she rigged herself. Whenever she crammed folks into her teeny place, she folded it up against a wall with the help of shower-curtain hooks and rods, concealing the bulge of the mattress with blue-and-white tablecloths she found at Azuma, a Japanese schlock shop on Eighth Street next door to Brentano's, where I was employed as a bookseller. Otherwise, there was just a low rust-colored corduroy sofa Miguel and I had helped her lug from where he'd spotted it on Avenue B, near the park, plus some overstuffed pillows strewn across the linoleum floor.

FOOLS FOR LOVE **5**

On nonperformance nights, when we brought Stromboli's pizzas upstairs in cardboard boxes, we were a family: the three of us with our similar-sounding last names—I'd taken Miguel's at the City Clerk's Office in Lower Manhattan, no way was I holding on to Lipschutz—and completely different origin stories. Usually we were joined by whomever Hattie was dating at the time: boys, girls, it didn't matter, it was "the person" that counted to Hattie. We'd spread a big beach towel out on her floor like a picnic table, drink Soave Bolla out of Dixie cups, and eat hard, sandy Italian cookies from Veniero's bakery, my favorites bejeweled by maraschino cherries.

On performance nights like this one, she arranged the various forms of seating in a tight semicircle around "the stage," an empty blank white box of nothingness otherwise known as Hattie's kitchen. In a corner of the room was her ancient refrigerator, which tended to buzz at precisely the wrong time, a sink, a little wooden bar cart that housed her coffeemaker, toaster oven, and hot plate. Sometimes, Hattie invited poets to read. Occasionally playwrights like me used the room to workshop stuff.

Already, as I settled into my window seat, the spritely, generous Hattie was starting the evening as she always did: with a little song she wrote and played on her ukulele. Hattie had no real talent to speak of, beyond the curatorial—which I now know is *everything*. I didn't realize what a Petri dish "the Square" was until a bunch of us just kept on working after getting our start there, and a few folks became famous.

Then she introduced the show. For months, Miguel and his best friend from boyhood, Angel, both Dominicans from

6 FOOLS FOR LOVE

Washington Heights, had been working on a same-sex performance of an abridged version of Sam Shepard's masterful new play, *Fool for Love.* An actor friend had snuck them a script, and in their buoyant and budding hubris they futzed around with it, with an eye on giving Angel, openly gay, a role to shine in. The show had by this time premiered in San Francisco and Shepard had already won a Pulitzer for something else, but that didn't stop these two from having their fun. His play was about a pair of lovers, Eddie and May, who find out well into their romance—which began as teenagers— that they have the same biological father. Hearing this news, Eddie's mother kills herself, and the kids break up. Years later, Eddie, still heartbroken, tracks May down to a motel room in the Mojave Desert to win her back.

The lights dimmed and three men entered the stage from the greenroom of Hattie's loo. My Miguel, in his best James Dean white T-shirt and a borrowed motorcycle jacket, was the tortured Eddie. The Murphy bed was open and neatly made. That and two of the folding chairs were the lone props. Angel, dressed like a carhop on roller skates (a nod to Shepard's earlier *The Tooth of Crime*), wore white leather rhinestone shorts and a white mesh top. He was May, although for purposes of this production, they had changed his name to Max, and he executed a series of graceful figure eights before rolling to the kitchen sink to begin washing dishes. In Shepard's original script, the father was identified only as "the Old Man," and this evening he was played by an older Brit—by which I mean *older than us,* nearing thirty— who was also the director. This guy, a "total fox," as we used

FOOLS FOR LOVE **7**

to say, with teal-colored eyes and long, long legs, sat to the side of the stage in one of the folding chairs, wearing worn denim overalls, a plaid flannel shirt, and a fishing hat (as if that touch of Americana might cancel out his accent). As per the text, he commented throughout the play.

But it was Miguel who had the kickoff, laying out Eddie and Max's history: *It was like we knew each other from somewhere but we couldn't place where. But the second we saw each other, that very second, we knew we'd never stop being in love.*

He was talking about Angel's character but looking directly at me, giving a little wink. I winked back; he did this once a show. Always. It was our "thing," because the first time we'd laid eyes upon each other on the train, back in high school, he'd leaned across the subway car and said: "What fucks like a tiger and winks?" And then blinked both his eyes silly. We'd laughed back then, and even now, six years later, it still undid me.

Then Miguel strode onto center stage, just as Angel turned away from the sink to dry his hands on a paper towel. The look on Angel/Max's face when he saw Miguel/Eddie in his home!

Miguel said: *He's just standing there, staring at me and I'm staring back at him, and we can't take our eyes off each other.*

Then Miguel moved toward poor Angel. *I came to see if you were all right,* he said.

I don't need you! Angel cried out.

Okay, Miguel said. *Fine,* and he started to walk away.

Angel, in agony, screamed: *DON'T GO!*

With that they rushed into each other's arms. In victory,

Miguel actually appeared to levitate off the ground. And there it was, the anguish and joy genuine passion created, the toing and froing, the losing and winning—at this point in my life I don't know if I'd wish it on anyone, but back then there was no denying the jealousy and exhilaration we in the audience felt while witnessing their A-train-coming-at-you brand of forbidden love. Who wouldn't want a piece of that sexy, hot, rapturous action if they could have it, even momentarily, no matter what the cost? They were so goddamned alive in each other's arms!

That's what I adore about the theater. It was realer than real life. It told the truth no one could convey in an article or essay or even in a Dear John letter. It's not like I was an idiot or Miguel was a liar. Au contraire. We told each other *everything*! We were soulmates. And we were fools. But what I saw on that stage in Hattie's apartment was two boys desperately in love, so ready to fuck there and then I could literally picture it in my mind's eye.

I was crying when Hattie hit the light switch at the close of the show (the Square had no curtains), and clapping thundered throughout the apartment, the iridescent bubble that I'd blown around my life punctured and now impossible to reconstruct. Before it was revealed to me through live theater, our marriage arrangement had somehow felt negligible, even deniable, something theoretical and insubstantial that I could brush aside. Never in my whole life have I ever understood anything that was not presented to me on a silver platter of narrative. You could put a message on a billboard on Broadway, up in lights, but it wouldn't sink in unless I arrived

FOOLS FOR LOVE **9**

at it through the transformative journey of a well-enacted story.

I was crying, but also I felt nauseous. I thought, I must be getting my period—maybe I'm just feeling hormonal? Because disavowal and acceptance were paradoxically my drugs of choice. Until they weren't. When Hattie turned the lights back up again, I made a beeline for the restroom as all three performers, now receiving a standing O, were taking their well-earned bows. I had to push through the crowd and cut across a corner of the stage to get there.

Hattie's bathroom. It was the same water closet that the actors had stepped away from and, in Angel's case, *rolled* out of just ninety minutes earlier. I opened the door, turned on the light, and closed it behind me. Hattie's toothbrush and toothpaste sat in a little plastic cup on the dated olive-green enamel sink. I swiped a tampon from the box I knew she kept in the medicine chest. After I inserted it, flushed the paper applicator, and began to wash my hands and tearstained face, I looked hard at myself in that oxidizing mirror: I was pretty in a way most girls are for a time when they are young. I had a mild eating disorder, which was looking good on me. Ellen Stewart at La MaMa had agreed just the week before to produce my newest one act. What was I whining about? My husband and I were made for each other. We snuck into Broadway plays during intermission, danced together at Hurrah, listened to music at Max's Kansas City, played pool in the neighborhood bars, and stayed up all night talking about the sun, moon, and stars. Most important, he read every single page I ever wrote and improved them almost all of the time. I'd never felt that understood or supported by anyone else in my entire life. So what, he liked to sleep with men?

I did, too.

This had all been discussed and understood between us since the twelfth grade. I, also, could have sex with whomever I chose, although he didn't like it when I did, and I didn't want to—and anyway Miguel and I were still lovers, he was enough for me, he knew how to get me off and he did it willingly and, I'd thought at the time, with some pleasure (although he preferred me on my stomach). He just did other things with other people once in a while because I wasn't enough for him. No one's fault but God's, whom Miguel believed in; he was Catholic and that is why we married. (I was a secular Jew from Stuyvesant Town whose parents thought I'd lost my mind. They were still hoping I'd get back together with my sixth-grade boyfriend, a boy named David Hershleder, who went from Bronx Science straight to Cornell University and was headed in the fall to Mount Sinai medical school. *Hershleder* was the ideal son-in-law!)

Looking in the mirror, I'd almost convinced myself that all this was true—easy, because it was—and that it was also sustainable (I can feel you rolling your eyes), and, while I was practicing the art of self-deception, that I, too, like Sam Shepard, would win a Pulitzer if I finally wrote a play with three full acts, when the British director barged into the bathroom without knocking.

"Sorry, but I really need to wee," he said.

"Don't let me stop you," I said.

He reached into the fly of his overalls, whipped it out, and aimed straight into the toilet. "I was practically swimming out there."

He'd played the nasty Old Man kind of stiffly, I thought, but then again, he wasn't supposed to be an actor. He was the director, the director who coaxed that magnificent performance out of my Miguel. In thirty more awkward seconds I would learn his name was Walker, and after he buttoned up and politely washed his hands, he shook mine and introduced himself.

"Anna," I said.

Then I turned the bathroom knob and we exited together.

Miguel and Angel were grinning maniacs standing in the middle of the set with their arms around each other's shoulders, like ballplayers after a winning game surrounded by a circle of glowing fans. Miguel was on his tippy-toes, telescoping his neck (shortness being his singular physical imperfection), clearly searching the room.

"Anna," he shouted, waving me over and giving Walker the stink eye. "Where have you been? What were you two doing in there? Not coke, I hope, without me."

What choice did I have then but to run to him? It was my job as his wife, his muse! He let go of Angel and swung me around in the air in a little circle, the skirt of my dress billowing, like everything about us, dramatically.

"What did you think, *mi amor*?" he asked.

"You were so amazing!" I said.

"You liked it?" he whispered in my hair. "It was all for you. For us." And then he smiled. "And a little bit for Angel."

"I did, I did," I said while he pulled back and held me at arm's length to see if I was telling the truth. My opinion was of the utmost importance to him. "You were great. He was good. But you were truly spectacular."

"I love you so much," he said. "Every day I ask God, How did I get this lucky?"

"I love you, too," I said.

Then he put one crazy macho arm possessively around my shoulders. I could smell his underarm when he reached over behind my head, his Old Spice, and the musk of him, like when he ran, or when we had sex; he was painted in sweat from the performance. "I see you've met my wife," he said to Walker.

"Anna?" said Walker, his eyebrows shooting up in cartoonish surprise.

Just then, Hattie's refrigerator loudly buzzed like a timer on a game show. Everyone turned to look at it, and then everyone turned back to look at Walker.

"Well, I guess I have met your wife," Walker said, regaining his footing.

"What were the two of you doing together in the bathroom?" Miguel asked again. Suddenly we were back at the basketball courts in Fort Tryon Park, surrounded by the Bichos, his tough-guy crew from high school. It was another thing I loved about him—how easily he got territorial and possessive.

"I really had to go," said Walker, shrugging. "I didn't realize someone was already in there."

"We met cute," I said, hoping to sound flip.

FOOLS FOR LOVE **13**

There was a fizzy little blonde in a polka-dot mini and one of those fuzzy sweaters, standing impatiently next to Angel.

"Anna, this is Jeannie Elbazz," Miguel introduced us. "She's an agent. She reps Jake Kamins."

I knew the name. Jeannie's. Jake's, too. He'd been in all those Oliver Stone movies. Clearly, so did Walker.

He stuck out his hand. "Walker Cogdill," he said.

"Nice job *directing*," said Jeannie, meaningfully. I guessed she too didn't think much of his acting ability. Then she turned to me, "Do you mind if I borrow your hubby for the rest of the evening? I've been invited to a little industry party and there are some people I'd like for him to meet."

Walker and Angel released a collective sigh of defeat.

"No, I don't mind," I said, in wifely mode. "Walker and Angel and I were planning on getting dinner anyway." Why on earth did I say that? That's the last thing I wanted. I wanted to go home. Kiss my Siamese cat, Buster. Put on Joni Mitchell. Cry my eyes out in the shower. Smoke a joint and call Hattie and talk to her until either Miguel arrived or we both fell asleep on the phone.

"Lo siento, querida," Angel said to me. "I'm going dancing with the fairies." He pointed to his posse waiting patiently in the corner. One of them was his official boyfriend, Bobby. He was the first to get sick, although he lived long enough to go on AZT.

"I'd be happy to dine with you," said Walker.

Jeannie was already glancing with impatience at her watch.

Miguel looked at me with his big dark eyes, searchingly.

He was sweet that way. He wanted to make sure I was okay. The cynical among you may accuse me of looking back through the rosy gold of a nostalgic haze, but I'm not sure anyone else, be they parent or lover or friend, has ever been as attentive to my feelings as he was.

"Go," I said. "Go." We kissed goodbye and I gave Jeannie a little wave, but she was already heading out the door and Miguel was loping across the floor to catch up with her.

Then I turned to Walker. "You really don't have to," I said.

"This is my very first American gig," said Walker. "It's either I eat with you, or I get a couple of slices by my lonesome and go home and watch the telly."

"Do you like Szechuan cold sesame noodles?" I asked him. They were the rage in those days and super cheap.

"That's Chinese, hmm? New to me," said Walker. "But new to me is why I'm here. I'm game. Also, I'm pretty fucking hungry."

"Bamboo House," I said. "The sign says Chinese and Japanese food, but it's really just sesame oil and peanut butter. However, they serve free wine. Just over on Second Avenue."

"Free wine, you say?" said Walker. "I'm sold. You lead the way."

"Okay," I said. "But first I have to go thank Hattie."

. . .

It took me another thirty minutes or so to extricate myself from the Square, there were so many cheeks to kiss, compliments to collect, and joints to toke. As I finally made it to the door, that guardian angel Hattie offered sotto voce, "If you want to come back after, Annie, we can have a sleepover," and I nodded, feeling a little teary again.

So I was surprised to find Walker waiting patiently for me on the sidewalk when I finally made my exit. I was sure he was long gone, but there he was drinking a beer. When I hopped off the last stoop step onto the street, he produced another bottle for me from the cargo pocket of his overalls.

"I know these dungarees seem a bit sad," he said, staring down at his pathetic outfit. "But they are in the stage directions. I got you a Heineken. Sorry if it's warm as piss."

"It took me too long to get out of there," I said. "My fault. Are you still up for this?"

"Stop asking that," said Walker. "It's embarrassing. I have nothing else to do, and I'm grateful for the company."

We started walking over to Second Avenue, past the little Catholic school on the left, and Cafe Mogador, where they still have belly dancing, I'm told, on the right. The sidewalk was crowded because that night was just getting started.

"So how long have you and Miguel been hitched?"

He grabbed my waist as I was about to step in a little Carvel curl of dog doo, and swung me past it, just by lifting me off the ground an inch or two. The man was taller and stronger than I'd thought at first blush.

"Three years," I said. "But we've been together six. We did it after my freshman year at The New School."

"Good for you. Though you don't look old enough to be married to anyone," said Walker.

"Well, I am," I said, defiantly.

"Your other half is brilliant," he said, then, starting over, unadorned admiration leaking out his mouth, "As a director, I never want to tell the actors what to do, I want to wheedle it out of them, it's more organic that way, but I didn't have to sweet-talk Miguel. He's the real deal, a natural. More than that, I think he will go far."

I swelled with pride, out of habit.

We turned the corner; Bamboo House was down the middle of the block. "That's it," I said, pointing to the neon sign in the plate-glass window.

"'Exotic food,'" Walker read out loud. "I guess the free wine isn't enough of a selling point?"

He opened the door and walked right in. Well trained by his loving mama, Miguel always held the door for me. To his credit, Walker sidestepped and held it ajar with one foot. We were seated in a vinyl booth by the window, bordered by snake plants on the sill, red lanterns hanging above our heads. A busy Chinese man wearing a white paper hat placed a teapot and two cups on the Formica table. Chopsticks and forks. Then he handed us menus that had been tucked under one arm. Walker opened his. "What should I have?" he asked.

"Egg rolls, barbecued ribs, fried rice?" Those were Miguel's favorites.

"Done," said Walker and closed it again.

"What? I was just listing some family favorites. I'm not so sure how balanced a meal that is."

"Well, I'm famished. And we're also getting the peanut macaroni right?" he said. "Then I think this should be enough."

I looked at the menu and remembered my eating disorder. "I'm getting some brown rice and steamed broccoli," I said.

"And I'll let you eat my noodles," he said, like it was settled. I relaxed a little.

The waiter came back with two cold glasses of fetchingly toxic-looking wine—they were an unnatural shade of Crayola lemon yellow—and placed them on the table. He took out his guest-check pad, and Walker nodded at me, so I did the ordering for both of us.

"What about you?" I asked, once the waiter was out of earshot. "Do you have someone special in your life?" I sounded like my great-aunt Sadie.

"Holly? She's a ballerina," he said. "She's dancing with the Royal Ballet right now. She's supposed to come visit this summer if I last that long."

"Why did you come to New York?" I asked. I took a sip of the wine. It was as sweet and thirst quenching as Kool-Aid. I liked it. It went down easy, and when the waiter passed by, I motioned for another round, even though I hadn't finished this one yet. By the time he came back with the food, I'd want it.

"I can do things here I can't do back in London. Like tonight for instance. Like, I also like to stage dance, which is how Holly and I met. I'm not afraid of mixing stuff up," he said. "Music, dance, theater, art, it's all the same to me. Together, it's only more interesting."

"I write plays myself," I said. "It's the only thing I can do, period. I mean, I work in a bookstore and I'm slowly, slowly creeping toward my BA, but I'd be a disaster at an office job, or anything else grown-up."

The waiter plopped two new glasses of wine on the table—as if they had been prepoured on a conveyor belt in the kitchen. Finally, Walker took a tiny sip from his first one.

"This stuff is nasty," he said, making a face.

"Oh no," I said, chugging mine. "We could order you a beer?"

"Nah." He smiled. "It's like this neighborhood. Sweet, cheap, and nasty. I'm thrilled to be here." And indeed, he looked thrilled.

"So what is Holly like?" I asked.

"She's fabulous. Beautiful, talented, smart, kind . . ." He trailed off a little.

"But?" I said.

He shook his head and frowned. "I'm not sure I love her enough," he said.

"I don't have that problem," I said.

"Oh no?" he asked, arching an eyebrow. "You and Miguel?"

"If anything, I love him too much," I said.

"I'm quoting the master himself now," Walker said. "'Love is the only disease that makes you feel better.' Sam Shepard said that in an interview I read. I have fun with Holly, I like her a lot, but I don't know if she makes me feel better."

Did Miguel make me feel better? In some very important ways he did, the ones I'd thought, until this particular night, mattered most. But in one really important way he made me feel small and lonely.

The waiter came back with a big tray. All of our fried, carby, greasy food at once. He served the dishes around the table like a croupier. Everything was sizzling.

"I want to be in love like that," Walker said, digging into

the big bowl of sesame noodles with his fork and plopping a mountain of it on my plate.

"Me, too," I said. "I mean, I want that for you." Showily, using my chopsticks, I took a big, delicious bite.

"And I want that for you, too," he said. Which startled me; hadn't I just said that was what I already had? I looked up straight into his teal-blue eyes and I felt the power of his stare travel all the way through my brown ones and down my spine and shiver into my knees. What the fuck?

. . .

After dinner, Walker walked me back to Hattie's. I lied and told him that I'd left something behind, a purse or a hat, my pet poodle? Something that made no sense at all; I didn't want him to know that I was going to sleep at Hattie's because I figured Miguel would sleep at Angel's, but I don't think Walker was paying too much attention by then. He looked tired. And maybe a little drunk and sick from all that oily food and crappy wine.

When we got to Hattie's stoop, I asked him where he was staying. "With some lads I know from university, they have an apartment up on Fourteenth." He nodded to the north with his handsome head. And then he said, "You know it's rare to find someone so easy to talk to."

Was it? Maybe it was. I'd never dated anyone but Miguel, and he could chat up the moon. I didn't know what to say. So I nodded in agreement and tucked away the thought for later.

"Good night, then," he said, leaning over and kissing me on the cheek.

"Good night," I said, my heart a wild bird trapped inside my chest as I turned and raced up the mountain of steps leading to Hattie's apartment.

The door was unlocked. And who did I find splayed out on Hattie's Murphy bed, but my Miguel. He was reading a copy of *The Village Voice*.

"Hey, you," he said, sitting up and swinging his legs over the edge to rest his feet on the floor.

"Hey, you," I said. "Where's the Hat-ster?"

"She went out with Emile and them. She told me you were coming back here later, so I waited." He patted the bed next to him. I walked over and sat down.

"How was the party?" I asked.

"Pretty cool," Miguel said. "I think that Jeannie wants to sign me."

"That's awesome, Miguel," I said, throwing my arms around him.

He laughed and hugged me back, allowing me to snuggle down into my space under his left arm, near the armpit.

"How was dinner with Walker?" he said.

"He's a nice guy," I said.

"He's a good director," Miguel said. He leaned over and tipped my face up, so I had to look him in the eyes.

He pushed some of my curls behind one of my ears. "I hope tonight wasn't too much for you," he said.

He never had any intention of hurting me, I'm telling you that now sincerely. Nobody loved each other more than me and Miguel. Love was not our problem.

"It was and it wasn't," I said.

"You are my precious wife," he said.

"And you are my darling husband," I said.

Then we lay back on the bed in each other's arms and guess what? We fell asleep that way, both of us with our clothes and boots still on, like little kids. Around 3:00 a.m., Hattie came home, and she crawled into the bed with us. I was aware enough of her to roll over and hand her part of the duvet. As I said, in those days, the Herreras and Hattie Henderson were a family.

There are nights that take you from A to C and nights that take you from A to Z. This night took me from A to W, to Walker. I mean not right away, of course, but eventually. Inevitably. It was a slow and painful reckoning. And for me, a big motherfucking surprise! I know I thought something incredible was coming when I'd left Brentano's earlier that evening, but never did I think it would take me away from the man I loved with all my heart.

Sometimes it requires forever to act on what you've already known for a long, long time. I suppose it was a little like quitting heroin, the highs, the lows, the anguish and the hunger. Walker waited patiently in the friend zone, until after a while, Miguel was either on the road working, or he was "out" all the time. Crying on Walker's shoulder when Miguel didn't come home one evening led us to making love on Walker's futon in his apartment. What can I say? It was revelatory. Finally, I was enough for someone else.

"More than enough," Walker whispered into my ear that night. "You are more than enough for me."

When I got the courage to move out of our place and into Hattie's, a protesting Miguel still helped me carry my belongings over to Saint Mark's. Little lambs that we were, we sobbed ceaselessly in each other's arms, not realizing a sadder day was coming.

In the meanwhile, Jeannie had been doing her job, thank God. Miguel had a great run after *Fool.* He went on the road as Horst in *Bent;* in *Biloxi Blues* he played Eugene, with Jake Kaminsky as Arnold; and with his inky-black locks dyed sandy brown, he took the crown as Biff in *Death of a Salesman* on Broadway. During that time he'd likewise moved on from Angel to Angel's ex Bobby, and then to Marcos. I'd left, but I'd also set him free! There was a new kind of harmony then, between us.

It was another year before Miguel tested positive. It took encouragement and hand-holding from Walker to get tested myself, so we did it together. I was shaking when they drew my blood, but Walker held me steady. When it was his turn, he just stuck out his arm.

With that out of the way, we moved in together into a Mitchell-Lama sublet on First Ave and Second Street.

Angel eventually gave up on theater and entered the world of fashion and is alive today. As Miguel got sicker, Angel and I and Miguel's mother took turns taking care of him. We hadn't divorced, and even if we had, he would always be my husband. Sometimes Walker would accompany me to the apartment, and sometimes when I was working, he also went on his own to visit. They were friends, in the end. As Miguel lay dying, I sat by his bedside, day after day after day, the two of us talking a blue streak like always. Once he stopped eating, the conversations stopped, too, Miguel's eyes glazing as I read to him from his beloved Auden, from the *New York Post*. I sang to him until, one evening, after he had long stopped saying much, he'd shaken his ravaged head, bald and spotted, unrecognizable, and said, "*Mi amor, por favor,* please, please, shut up." It was almost as if he'd come back from the dead. We burst out laughing. We laughed and laughed, our final laugh together.

I'm the worst singer in the world.

After Miguel died, Walker and I kept on working and building our careers. Eventually, we put a ring on it, and had a little daughter. Kate. She is the light of both our lives. But from time to time, usually in the darkness of one of those sleepless nights of the midnight soul, I'll text my old pal Hattie Henderson. She's a mother of three now and lives a stay-at-home life in some shmancy town in Westchester—a lot's changed, but a lot hasn't. She is still my unpaid confessor. Like last night, when I wrote to her at two o'clock in the morning: *Did you know I was fucking nuts back then?*

Hattie was up, too. Like me, she has demons no amount of bourgeois posturing can shake. At 2:15 she texted back: *Everyone did! But all of us were kind of nuts then too.*

I wrote back: *Don't tell. It would kill Walky, but sometimes I still miss Miguel so much I bite down on my own fist until it bleeds.*

There were little red pearls pooling on my knuckles. I stanched them with torn pieces of Kleenex the way Walker did when he cut his neck shaving.

Hattie texted back: *You were meant for each other in a better place. Here on earth, it all pretty much sucks. Even though a lot of things are beautiful.*

I looked at my hand and saw that the bleeding had stopped.

So I crawled back into bed and closed my eyes.

THE
REVISIONIST

I t had been a hundred years since Hershleder had taken in a late-afternoon movie, a hundred years since he had gone to the movies by himself. It was 5:45. There was a 6:15 train Hershleder could still make. But why give in and do something as inevitable as being home on time for dinner? At heart he was a rebel. Hershleder walked up the avenue to a revival house in Kips Bay. He could enter the establishment in daylight. When was the last time he had done that, gone from a dazzling summer afternoon—when the air was visible and everything looked like it was in a comic book, only magnified, broken down into a sea of shimmering dots—into the dark, cool mouth of an air-conditioned hall? It was a dry July day. It was hot out. Who cared what was playing? Porno. Action. Comedy. All Hershleder wanted was to give himself over to something.

He was drawn to the box office as if the gum-chewing bored girl behind the counter were dispensing pharmaceutical cocaine and he was still a young and reckless intern—the kind he had always planned on being, the kind Hershleder was only in his dreams. She had big hair. Brown hair, sprayed and teased into wings. She had a dark mole beneath her pink lips on the left-hand side of her face. It looked like the period that marks a dotted quarter in musical notation. She was a beautiful girl in an interesting way. Which means if the light were right (which it wasn't quite then), if she held her chin at a particular angle (which she didn't, her chin was in a constant seesaw on account of the gum) when she laughed or when she forgot about pulling her lips over her teeth (which were long and fine and—at the most reductive—canine), she was a lovely cubist vision.

Hershleder bought two tickets out of force of habit. He entered the building, passed the two tickets toward the ticket taker, and realized that he was alone.

Back at the box office, the girl wouldn't grant Hershleder a refund. She said: "It's a done deal, dude." But she smiled at him.

Hershleder gave the extra ticket to a bag lady who sat under the marquee where the sidewalk was slightly more shaded than the street, where the open and close of the glass doors to this refrigerated cinema provided the nearest thing to an ocean breeze that she would feel on this, her final face.

Hershleder the blind, Hershleder the dumb—oblivious to the thrill of a beautiful big-haired girl's lyrical smile, a smile a musician could sight-read and play. Blind and stuck with an extra ticket, Hershleder gave it away to the old lady. He wasn't a bad guy, really. Hadn't the old woman once been somebody's baby? Wasn't it possible, also, that she was still somebody's mother? Were there ever two more exalted roles in human theater? This woman had risen to the pinnacle of her being, and she'd fallen. She suffered from La Tourette. Hershleder held the glass door open for her; he'd been well raised by his own mother, a woman with a deep residing respect for the elderly.

"Bastard," said the old lady, smiling shyly. "Cocksucker."

Hershleder smiled back at her. Here was someone who spoke his language. Hadn't he seen a thousand and one patients like her before?

"Nazi prick," the woman said, her voice trailing low as she struggled to gain control of herself. Her face screwed up in concentration; she wrestled with her inner, truer self. "Cocksucker," she said through clenched teeth; she bowed her head now, trying to direct her voice back into her chest. The next word came out like an exhalation of smoke, in a puff, a whisper: "Motherfucker."

The old lady looked up at Hershleder from beneath hooded lids—in her eyes was a lifetime of expressions unfortunately not held back, of words unleashed, epithets unfettered—there was a locker room of vile language in her head, but her face seemed apologetic. When Hershleder met her gaze, she fluttered her lashes, Morse-coding like the end-stage ALS patient on Ward A, then turned and shuffled away from him.

. . .

It was delicious inside the auditorium. Cold enough for Hershleder to take off his jacket and lay it flat like a blanket across his lap. His hand wandered across his crotch, stroked his belly. In the flirtation of film light, Hershleder felt himself

28 FOOLS FOR LOVE

up under the curtain of his outerwear. There were a couple of teenagers in the back of the house who talked throughout the movie, but what did Hershleder care? It was dark, there was music. Stray bits of popcorn crunched beneath his feet. A side door opened, and he got high off the smell of marijuana wafting on a cross breeze. An old man dozed in an end seat across the aisle. A beautiful girl on-screen displayed a beautiful private birthmark. A bare-chested man rolled on top of her, obscuring Hershleder's view. Above, warplanes flew, bombs dropped, the girl moaned, fire fire fire. Something was burning. On-screen? Off-screen? The exit sign was the reddest thing he'd ever seen. It glowed on the outskirts of his peripheral vision. Time passed in a solid leap, as in narcotized sleep, as in coma. When the lights came up, Hershleder was drowsily aware that much had happened to him—but what? Couldn't the real world have jumped forward at the rate of on-screen time, in quantum leaps of event and tragedy and years? The movies. Like rockets hurtling a guy through space.

It was a way to make the hours pass, that's for sure, thought Hershleder. For a moment he had no clue as to what day it was.

. . .

Grand Central Station.

Hershleder waited for information. On the south wall was a huge photo essay, Kodak presenting the glories of India. A half-naked child, his brown outstretched hand, an empty bowl, his smile radiant. A bony cow. A swirl of sari, a lovely face, a red dot like a jewel amid the light filigree of a happy forehead. A blown-up piece of poori: a bread cloud. The Taj Mahal . . . *In All Its Splendor.*

The lobby of Bellevue Hospital looked something like the concourse did below this gussied-up fairy-tale display. Women in rags, homeless beggars, drug addicts that punctuated the station like restless exclamation marks. Inge, his chief lab technician, had told him that at the hospital, in the ground-floor bathrooms, mothers bathed their babies in the sinks. Hershleder could believe this. There, like here, was a place to come in out of the cold, the rain, the heat.

The signboard fluttered its black lids; each train announcement inched its way up another slot. Hershleder's would depart from Track 11. There was time for half a dozen oysters at the Oyster Bar. He headed out past Zaro's bakery, the bagels and the brioche, the pies with mile-high lemon meringue. Cholesterol—how it could slather the arteries with silken ecstasy! (Hershleder had to watch himself. Oysters would do the trick—in more ways than one. What was that old joke . . . the rules of turning forty: Never waste an erection, never trust a fart?) He hung a left, down the curved, close passageway—the tunnel that felt like an inner tube, an underground track without the track, an alimentary canal, a cool stone vagina. Vagrants sagged against the walls, sprawled beneath the archways. There was a souvenir stand. A bookstore. A florist! Daisies, bright white for Itty, beckoned from earthenware vases. This was a must-stop on his future trek to Track 11. The passageway smelled like a pet store. The horrible inevitable decay of everything biological, the waste, the waste! Hershleder did a little shocked pas de bourrée over a pretzel of human shit, three toe steps, as lacy as a dancer's.

. . .

They slid down easy, those Wellfleets, Blue Points. Hershleder leaned against the polished wood and ordered another half dozen. Not liquid, not solid—a fixed transitional state. A second beer. So what if he missed his train? There would always be another. Death and taxes. The Harlem and the Hudson Lines. The fact that oysters made him horny.

They slid down cold and wet. Peppery. Hershleder wasn't one to skimp on hot sauce. The shell against his upper lip was blue and smooth, his lower lip touched lichen, or was it coral? Pinstripes made up his panorama. The other slurpers were all like him. Commuters. Men who traveled to and from their wives, their children, "the Office." Men with secret lives in a foreign land: the city. Men who got off on eating oysters, who delayed going home by having yet another round of drinks. They all stood in a row at the bar the way they would stand at a row of urinals. Each in his private world. "Aaach," said Hershleder, and tipped another briny shell to his lips. His mouth was flooded by ocean.

Delays, delays. A lifetime full of delays. Hershleder the procrastinator, the putter-offer. Hershleder of the term papers started the night before, the grant proposals typed once into the computer, the postmarks fudged by the hospital's friendly postmaster. He was the kind of man to leave things to the last minute, to torture himself every moment that he did not attend to what needed attending to, his tasks, but also the type always to get them done. While in his heart he lusted after irresponsibility, he was never bad enough. Chickenshit. A loser.

Hershleder's neighbor at the bar was reading *The New York Times*.

"Hey, mister," said Hershleder, sounding like he was seven. "Would you mind letting me look at the C section?" Now he spoke like a gynecologist.

The neighbor slid the paper over without even glancing up.

Hershleder turned to the book review.

David Josephson. His old pal from college. A picture of the sucker. A picture; why a picture? It wasn't even Josephson's book. That schlepp was just the translator!

Josephson had not fared well over time, although, to be fair, the reproduction was kind of grainy. A hook nose. A high forehead. He still looked brainy. That forehead hung over his eyes like an awning at a fancy club. Hershleder read the article for himself.

A 1,032-page study of the Nazi gas chambers has been published. . . . The study is by Jacques LeClerc, a chemist who began his work doubting that the Holocaust even took place. . . . The book, written in French (translated by that bald rat Josephson), . . . presents as proof, based entirely on technical analysis of the camps, that the Holocaust was every bit as monstrous and sweeping as survivors have said. . . . It is also a personal story of a scientific discovery during which, as Mr. LeClerc writes in a postscript, he was converted from "revisionist" to "exterminationist."

32 FOOLS FOR LOVE

Exterminationist. What a hell of an appellative. Hersh‑leder shook his head, in public, at the Oyster Bar, at no one in particular. Exterminationist. Is that what he himself was? His beloved mother, Adela Hershleder, just a child, along with her sister and her mother, her father recently dead of typhus, smuggled out of Germany on Kristallnacht. His mother's mother lost six brothers and sisters in Hitler's crematoria. And the friends, the extended family, even the neighbors they didn't like—all gone, gone. Hershleder's grandfather Chaim and his grandfather's brother, Abe, came to this country from Austria as refugees after World War I, the sole survivors of the sweeping tragedies of Europe that did away with their entire extended family.

And *heerre* . . . was Hershleder, the beneficiary of all that compounded survival; Hershleder the educated, the privileged, the beloved, the doctor! Hershleder the first-generation New York Jew, Hershleder the bar mitzvahed, the assimilated, Hershleder with the shiksa wife, the children raised on Christmas, bacon in their breakfast, mayonnaise spread across their Wonder bread, the daughter who once asked him if calling a person a Jew was really just another way to insult him.

He was lucky; his ancestors were not. What could you do? Wasn't this the crux of it all (the history of civilization): those of us who are lucky juxtaposed against those of us who are not?

Stacey and Lori, his sisters, married with children, each active in her own temple, one out on Long Island, one on the Upper West Side. Irv, his father, retired now, remarried now, donating his time to the Jewish Home for the Blind.

Were they any more Jewish than he was? Wasn't it true, what his own mother had told him, that what mattered in life was not religion per se but that one strived to be a good person? Wasn't he, Hershleder—the researcher and, on Tuesdays and Thursdays, the healer (albeit a reluctant one), the father, the husband, the lawn mower, the moviegoer (he did show that bag lady a good time), the friend to Josephson (at least in theory)—a good person?

My God, thought Hershleder, just imagine being this chemist, this LeClerc, having the courage to disprove the very tenets upon which you've built your life. But Hershleder knew this kind, he had seen them before: LeClerc's accomplishments were probably less about bravery than they were about obsessive compulsion: LeClerc was probably a man who practiced a strict adherence to facts, to science. After all, Hershleder had spent much of his adult life doing research. You let the data make the decisions for you. You record what you observe. You synthesize, yes, you interpret; but you don't theorize, create out of your own imagination, needs, and desires. He knew him, LeClerc, LeClerc the compulsive, the truth teller. They were alike, these two men, rational, exact, methodical. Science was their true religion. Not the ephemeral mumbo jumbo of politicians, philosophers, poets.

Hershleder and LeClerc: They told the truth, when they were able, when it stared them in the face.

Hershleder folded up the paper and left it on the counter, its owner, his neighbor, having vanished in the direction of the New Haven Line some time ago. Paid up and exited the comforts of the Oyster Bar and headed out into the fes-

34 FOOLS FOR LOVE

tering subterranean world. He stopped at the florist to pick up those daisies, two dozen, a field of them, a free-floating urban meadow. He held the bouquet like a cheerleader's pom-pom in his hands.

"Daisies are wildflowers," said the florist when he wrapped them up, those hothouse posies, in a crinkly paper cone. What did he think, that Hershleder had been a poster child for the Fresh Air Fund? He'd been to summer camp, away to college. Didn't he live in the suburbs and have a wife who cultivated daisies of her own? Daisies smell awful, but their faces are so sunny and bright, so fresh, so clean, petals as white as laundry detergent.

As he made his way to Track 11, Hershleder had a musical association: "Daisy, Daisy, give me your answer true." He had a poetic association: "She loves me, she loves me not." He had a visual association: the plastic daisy treads that his mother had stuck to the bottom of his bathtub so that he, Hershleder, her precious boy-child, the third born and most prized, wouldn't slip, hit his head, and drown. The big bright patent-leather daisies that adorned the thongs of his own daughter's dress-up sandals. The caramel yolk, the pinky white of Itty's eyes when she'd been crying.

Hershleder walked through the vaulted, starred amphitheater of Grand Central Station with a sensual garden, his human history, flowering bitterly in his hands.

· · ·

"Smoke," hissed a young man in a black concert T-shirt. "Thai stick, dust, coke." The young man stood outside

Track 11. Hershleder had seen this dealer there, this corrupter of the young and not so young, this drug pusher, almost every day for months and months. Hershleder nodded at him, started down the ramp to the train tracks, then stopped. He had been a good boy. At Bronx Science he had smoked pot, at Cornell he'd done magic mushrooms once in a while at a Dead show—then usually spent the rest of the night in the bathroom throwing up. For the most part, he'd played it safe: a little blow on a prom night or some graduation, but no acid, no ups, no downs (well, that wasn't true, there were bennies in med school, Valiums after), no needles in the arm, no track marks. No long velvety nights of swirling hazy rock songs. Drugwise, he was practically a virgin. Hadn't this gone on long enough?

Hershleder backtracked up the ramp.

"How much?" asked Hershleder.

"For what?" said Mr. Black Concert T-Shirt.

For what? For what?

"Heroin?" asked Hershleder, with hope.

Mr. Black Concert T-shirt looked away in disgust.

"Pot?" asked Hershleder humbly, in his place.

"Smoke," hissed the young man, "Thai stick, dust, coke."

"Thai stick," said Hershleder. Decisively. "Thai fucking stick," said Hershleder the reckless, the bon vivant.

And then, even though he was in danger of missing his train (again), Hershleder went back into the lobby of the station and bought cigarettes. He bought Merit Ultra Lights, thought better of it, backtracked to the kiosk and traded in the Merits for a pack of Salems.

36 FOOLS FOR LOVE

. . .

The john was small enough that if you were to sit your knees would be in your armpits and your elbows in your ears. Hershleder and his daisies floated in a cloud of smoke, mentholated, Asiatic (the Thai stick). The chemical smell of toilets on trains and airplanes permeated all that steam. The resultant odor was strong enough to etherize an elephant, but Hershleder the rebel was nose-blind to it. He was wasted.

The Metro-North rumbled through the tunnel. Outside, the scenery was so familiar Hershleder had it memorized. First the surprise of 125th Street, the hash of graffiti, of murals, loud paint. Then onward, the Bronx, Riverdale, Spuyten Duyvil. The scramble of weedy green, the lumberyards, factories, houses that line the train tracks in the suburbs. At night, all of this would be in shadow; what he'd see would be the advertisements for *Cats,* for Big Mac attacks, for Newport cigarettes: usually of a man gleefully dumping a bucket of something over an equally gleeful woman's head. The lonely maid still in uniform waiting for the train to carry her home two towns away. A couple of emasculated teenagers without driver's licenses. A spaced-out commuter who had stumbled off at the wrong station. Hershleder knew this route by heart.

In the train car itself, there was always the risk of running into one of his neighbors, or worse yet the aging parents of a pal from college. Better to hang out in that safe smoky toilet pondering the meaning of life, his humble existence. He was stoned for the first time in years. Drunken synapse fired awkwardly to drunken synapse. His edges were rounded, his reflexes dulled. The ghosts that lived inside him spiraled around in concentric circles. Hershleder's interior buzzed. His head hung heavy off his neck, rested in the field of daisies. A petal went up his nose, pollen dusted his mouth. He couldn't really think at all—he was full to the brim with nothing.

It was perfect.

"Laaarchmont," cried the lock-jawed conductor. "Laaarchmont," ruining everything.

. . .

Hershleder lit a cigarette and coughed up a chunk of lung. Larchmont. The station. A mile and a half from Casa Hershleder, a mile and a half from Itty and the kids, a mile and a half from his home and future heart failures. His eyes roved the commuter lot. Had he driven his car this morning or had Itty dropped him off at the train? Had he called for a cab, hitched a ride with a neighbor? Where was that beat-up Mazda? His most recent history dissolved like a photograph in water, a dream upon awakening, a computer screen when the power suddenly shuts down. It receded from his inner vision. Must have been the weed. It really knocked him out.

Good shit, thought Hershleder.

He decided to walk. What was a mile and a half? He was in the prime of his life. Besides, Hershleder couldn't arrive home like this, stoned, in front of his innocent children, his loving wife. A long stroll would surely be enough to sober him; it would be a head-clearing, emotional cup of coffee.

Larchmont. Westchester, New York. One curvy road segueing into another. A dearth of streetlights. The Tudor houses loomed like haunted mansions. They sat so large on their tiny lots, they swelled over their property lines the way a stout man's waist swells above his belt. A yuppie dog, a dalmatian, nosed its way across a lawn and accompanied Hershleder's shuffling gait. Hershleder would have reached down to pat its spotty head if he could have, but his arms were too full of daisies. He made a mental note to give in to Itty; she'd been begging him to agree to get a pup for the kids. There had been dogs when Hershleder was a child. Three of them. At different times. He had had a mother who couldn't say no to anything. He had had a mother who was completely overwhelmed. The longest a dog had lasted in their apartment in Stuyvesant Town had been about a year; Mrs. Hershleder kept giving those dogs away. Three dogs, three children. Was there some wish fulfillment involved in her casting them aside? His favorite one had been called Snoopy. A beagle. His sister Stacey, that original thinker, had been the one to name her.

Hershleder remembered coming home from camp one summer to find that Snoopy was missing. His mother had sworn up and down that she had given the dog to a farm, a farm in western Pennsylvania. Much better for the dog, said Mrs. Hershleder, than being cooped up in some tiny apartment.

Better for the dog, thought Hershleder now, some twenty-eight years later, better for the dog! What about me, a dogless boy cooped up in some tiny apartment! But his mother was dead, she was dead; there was no use in raging at a dead mother. Hershleder the motherless, the dogless, walked the streets of Larchmont. His buzz was beginning to wear off.

Why neurology? Mrs. Hershleder had asked. How about a little pediatrics? Gynecology? Family practice? Dovidil, don't make the same mistakes I made, a life devoted to half-lives, a life frozen in motion. But Hershleder had been drawn to the chronic ward. Paralysis, coma. He could not stand to watch a patient suffer, the kick and sweat, the scream of life battling stupidly for continuation. If he had to deal with people—and isn't that what a doctor does, a doctor deals with people—he preferred people in a vegetative state, he preferred them incognizant. What had attracted him in the first place had been the literature, the questions: What is death? What is life, after all? Do the answers to these lie, as Hershleder believed, not in the heart but in the brain? He liked to deal in inquiries; he didn't like to deal in statements. It was natural then that he'd be turned on by research. Books and libraries, the heady smell of ink on paper. He'd been the kind of boy who had always volunteered in school to run off things for the teacher. He'd stand close to the rexograph machine, giddy, greedily inhaling those toxic vapors. He'd walk back slowly to his classroom, his nose buried deep in a pile of freshly printed pages.

Hershleder was not taken with the delivering of babies, the spreading of legs, the searching speculum, the bloody afterbirth like a display of raw ground meat. But the brain, the brain, that fluted, folded mushroom, that lovely intricate web of thought and tissue and talent and dysfunction, of arteries and order. The delicate weave of neurons,

40 FOOLS FOR LOVE

that thrilling spinal cord. All that communication, all those nerves sending and receiving orders. A regular switchboard. Music for his mind.

A jogger passed him on the right, his gait strong and steady. Hershleder's dalmatian abandoned him for the runner.

Hershleder turned down Fairweather Drive. He stepped over a discarded red tricycle. He noticed that the Fishmans had a blue Jag in their carport. The Fishman boy was his own boy's nemesis. Charlie Fishman could run faster, hit harder. No matter that Hershleder's own boy could speak in numbers—a = 1, b = 2—for example, when Hershleder arrived home at night the kid said: "8-9, 4-1-4" (translation: Hi, Dad!); the kid was practically a savant, a genius! So what, the Fishman boy could kick harder, draw blood faster, in a fight. Could Charlie Fishman bring tears to his own father's eyes by saying, "9 12-15-22-5 25-15-21" when the Fishman father tucked him in at night? (Even though it had taken Hershleder seven minutes and a pad and pencil to decode the obvious.) Charlie Fishman had just beaten out Hershleder's Jonathan for the lead in the second-grade play. The Fishman father was a famous nephrologist. He commuted to New Haven every morning on the highway, shooting like a star in that blue Jag out of the neighborhood, against the traffic, in the opposite direction. Hershleder admired the Jag from afar. It was a blue blue. It glowed royally against the darkness.

The jogger passed him again, on the right. The dalmatian loped after the runner, his spotted tongue hanging from his mouth. The jogger must have circled around the long circuitous block in record time. A powerful motherfucker.

Bearded. And young. Younger than Hershleder. The jogger had a ponytail. It sailed in the current of his own making. His legs were strong and bare. Ropy, tendoned. From where he stood, Hershleder admired them. Then he moved himself up the block to his own stone Tudor.

Casa Hershleder. It was written in fake Spanish tile on the front walk, a gift from his sisters. Hershleder walked up the slate steps and hesitated on his own front porch. Sometimes it felt like only an act of courage could get him to turn the knob and go inside. So much tumult awaited. Various children: on their marks, getting set, ready to run, to hurl themselves into his arms. Itty, in this weather all soft and steamed and plumped—dressed in a tiered light blue cotton skirt and oversized whitish T-shirt—hungry for connection, attention, the conversation of a living, breathing adult. Itty, with tiny clumps of clay lodged like bird eggs in the curly red nest of her hair. Itty with the silt on her arms, the gray slip-like slippers on her bare feet. Itty, his wife, the potter.

By this point, the daisies were half dead. They'd wilted in the heat. Hershleder lay them in a pile on his front shrub, then lowered himself onto a slate-step seat. If he angled his vision past the O'Keefes' mock turret, he would surely see some stars.

The steam of summer nights, the sticky breath of the trees and their exhalation of oxygen, the buzz of the mosquitoes and the cicadas, the sweaty breeze, the rubbing of his suit legs against his thighs. The moon above the O'Keefes' turret was high, high, high.

The jogger came around again. Angled right and headed

up the Hershleder walk. His face was flushed with all that good clean high-octane blood that is the result of honest American exertion. He looked young—far younger than Hershleder—but hadn't Hershleder noted this before? Must be wanting to know the time, or in need of a glass of water, a bathroom, a phone, Hershleder thought. The jogger was jogging right toward him.

In a leap of blind and indiscriminate affection the dalmatian bounded past the runner and collided with Hershleder. David was stunned for a second, then revived by the wet slap of the dog's tongue. He was showered with love and saliva. "Hey," said Hershleder. "Hey there, buster. Watch it." Hershleder fended off the beast by petting him, by bowing under to all that animal emotion. The dalmatian wagged the bottom half of his spinal column like a dissected worm; it had a life all its own. His tail beat the air like a wire whisk. His tongue was as soft and moist as an internal organ.

"Hey, buster, down."

Hershleder's arms were full of dog.

The jogger jogged right past them. He wiped his feet on Hershleder's welcome mat. He opened Hershleder's door and entered Hershleder's house. He closed Hershleder's door behind him. There was the click of the lock Hershleder had installed himself. That old bolt sliding into that old socket.

What was going on? What was going on around here?

Buster was in love. He took to Hershleder like a bitch in heat, this same fancy mutt that had abandoned him earlier for the runner. A fickle fellow, thought Hershleder, a familiar fickle fellow.

"Hey," said Hershleder. "Hey," he called out. But it was too late. The runner had already disappeared inside his house.

The night was blue. The lawns deep blue green, the asphalt blue black, the trees almost purple. Jaundiced yellow light, like flames on an electric menorah, glowed from the Sullivans' leaded windows. At the Coens', from the second-floor family room, a TV flickered with a weak pulse. Most of the neighborhood was dark. Dark, sultry, blue, and yellow. A hot and throbbing bruise.

A car backfired in the distance. Buster took off like a shot.

Hershleder sat on his front step feeling used. He might as well have been a college girl left in the middle of a one-night stand. The dog's breath was still warm and wet upon his face. His clothes were damp and wrinkled. The smell of faded passion clung to him. His hair—what was left of it—felt matted. He'd been discarded. Thrown over. What could he do?

Stand up, storm into the house, demand: What's the meaning of this intrusion? Call the cops? Were Itty and the kids safe inside, locked up with that handsome, half-crazed stranger? Was it a local boy, home on vacation from college, an art student perhaps, hanging around to glean some of his wife's infinite and irresistible knowledge? The possibilities were endless. Hershleder contemplated the endless possibilities for a while.

Surely, he should right himself, climb his own steps, turn his key in his lock, at least ring his own bell, as it were. Surely, Hershleder should do something to claim what was his: *If I am not for me, who will be for me? If I am only for myself, what am I?* Surely, he should stop quoting, stop questioning, and get on with the messy thrill of homeownership. After all, his wife, his children, were inside.

The jogger was inside.

Hershleder and LeClerc, they told the truth when it stared them in the face. In the face! Which was almost enough but wasn't enough, right then at that exact and awful moment, to stop him, the truth wasn't, not from taking his old key out of his pocket and jamming it again and again at a lock it could not possibly ever fit. Which wasn't enough, this unyielding frustration, to stop him from ringing the bell, again and again, waking his children, disturbing his neighbors. Which wasn't enough to stop him, the confusion, the shouting that ensued, that led Itty, *his wife,* to say, "Please, sweetheart," to the jogger (Please, sweetheart!) and usher him aside, that ponytailed bearded athlete who was far, far younger than Hershleder had ever been, younger than was biologically possible.

She sat on the slate steps, Itty, her knees spread, the skirt pulled discreetly down between them. She ran her silt-stained hands through her dusty strawberry-blond cloud of hair. There were dark, dirty half-moons beneath her broken fingernails. She was brown-eyed and frustrated and terribly pained. She was beautiful, Itty, at her best really when she was most perplexed, her expression forming and re-forming like a kaleidoscope of puzzled and passionate emotion, when she patiently and for the thousandth time explained to him, Dr. David Hershleder, MD, that this was no longer his home, that the locks had been changed for this very reason. He had to stop coming around here, upsetting her, upsetting the children; it was time, it was time, Dave, to take a good look at himself; when all Hershleder was capable of looking at was her, Itty, dusty, plump, and sweaty, sexy-sexy Itty, his wife, his wife, sitting with him on the stoop of his house in his neighborhood, while his children cowered inside.

Until finally, exhausted (Hershleder had exhausted her), Itty threatened to call the police if he did not move, and it was her tiredness, her sheer collapsibility, that forced Hershleder to his feet—for wasn't being tired one thing Itty went on and on about that Hershleder could finally relate to, that pushed him to see the truth, to assess the available data, and to head out alone and ashamed and apologetic to his suburban slip of a sidewalk, down the mile and a half back to the station to catch the commuter rail that would take him to the city and to the medical student housing he'd wrangled out of the hospital, away from everything he'd built, everything he knew and could count on, out into everything unknown, unreliable, and yet to be invented.

THE
MEMOIRS
OF LUCIEN H.

From the get-go I am fabulous.

My first photo shoot is in utero. The image is etched in pure ivory, against a puddle of elegant black velvet, surrounded by a luscious backdrop of silver plush. No accessories per se, except for my heart, that tiny flicker, frozen on film like a classic diamond stud.

Vintage Jil Sander.

"What a little jewel," said Buster, my delicate, wide-eyed flower, just a kid herself and ruined now, barely a year off the bus. Weeping, she jumped off the gyno's table and hightailed it back to the garment center where everyone, from the designers to the cutters, oohed and aahed at my adorbs silhouette. Her boss, that old softy, made a frame out of a stray Manolo shoebox, and with much ceremony the entire studio pledged their undying support; Angel and Ira, who ran the front desk, dabbing at their eyes with a single Hermès scarf.

"Querido, never forget what Hillary taught us," Angel, the scarf's owner, said. "'It takes a village . . .'"

Verklempt, Ira chimed, "It sure does."

To cement their pledge to yours truly, they catered to

Buster by rubbing her shoulders and hands with various squirts and dabs of Aesop's—clashing scents rather recklessly if you ask me—and then laying a cool linen hankie across her white-blond brow. There was kombucha in the cupboard, and the receptionist ordered up pounds of veggie maki. Thus fêted and anointed, my mother was laid on a pink fainting couch, weeping out of fear (for she was only twenty-three and flat broke and she made her living off her figure, which was surely soon to go) as her fellow fit models hung the sonogram ceremoniously on the fridge.

Buster. A diminutive of Beatrice. Bestowed upon her by an older brother, Duke, who drank a quart of tequila and smashed into the barn with the family tractor. It was Duke's death that led my lady to take the next Trailways to New York. "You only live once," she said to herself, original thinking having never been her forte. She was voted "most likely to model" in her high school yearbook, and while that didn't exactly work out, her perfect size o frame led her to our studio where they cut Theory suits and dresses right off her narrow back.

I was the product of a Japanese tea ceremony with a Japanese photographer who then split for the Paris shows.

Sigh.

Now Buster does the books for better than minimum wage, as I permanently padded her hips, but my embryonic likeness is still up there on the fridge, and it is surrounded by my entire portfolio—me at three months, butt naked and pearly, belly down on a visiting designer's Celine Homme *fuhh;* me at six months, when the boss returned from a textile

48 FOOLS FOR LOVE

trip to Singapore, a little Panchen Lama in my hand-tailored suit of embroidered red and gold silks; me at nine months and finally upright, adorably clutching the platformed ankle of Hyacinth, a six-foot cover girl (catalogs). There is a veritable photo-essay of me! me! me! splayed across that SMEG 1950s-style retro FAB28 Veuve Clicquot special edition refrigerator, a fitting tribute to my sassy good looks, my round, amber eyes, the shock of my raven hair, inky as patent leather, many shades darker than my skin.

I am Lucien. Lucien H. to distinguish me from all the other Luciens in the playground. Center of the universe. Il Doge of the studio. King of the babies. This is my story, thus far.

Buster and I lived with a roommate—Jack, an unemployed actor (even I wouldn't cast him with that pizza face)—in a one-bedroom in Flatbush. Jack babysat Friday nights instead of rent whenever he came up short. Weekends were disastrous. Lonely Buster trolling the clubs until all hours hellbent on finding love. Eventually she'd end up back at our place with some finance bro dying to transmit his diseases. Mornings after began at eleven, when the asshole in question would inevitably chuck me under the chin on his way out and promise to text us later. Ha.

"We don't need him," Buster would whisper in my ear, her tears rolling down my neck. "We don't need anybody."

I heartily agreed with her.

Then she'd pull it together, for my sake, and we'd head out to Edie Jo's café and bar—French toast and cut-in-quarters grapes for me, Buster shaken but defiant, downing watermelon slushy after watermelon slushy, "a frozen marg," read the menu, heavy on the tequila. This was followed by a quick jaunt to the nearest sidewalk bench where we watched the pigeons shit—"Look at the poop!" said Buster. "Everybody poops!"—and we watched the rats play. Oh, my Buster. She was determined to be a good mother.

Sundays—hope springs eternal for Buster on a Sunday—we'd take the subway (the subway!) into Manhattan. We'd bumpety-bump my stroller up flight after flight of those subway stairs and no one would offer to lend a hand. We'd stroll over to an East Side playground in the ritziest of neighborhoods, home of Lucien B. and Lucien W., Luke and Lukie and Luciano, and all their respective daddies. The rest of the week, the playground belonged to nannies.

"There is nothing sexier than a rich man with a baby," said Buster, but, alas, we always came up short.

Weekdays, however, were sublime. Every weekday of my life, my bleary-eyed mama would slap a diaper on me, then dose me with a hearty slug of Similac, and wrap me in a blanket. A car-service car, sent by the boss, stood waiting to take us both to the garment center. Once in the studio, I was properly bathed while Buster picked at her bagel, the entire crew fussing over my morning toilette.

Bottom line: I never wore the same outfit twice.

That's not true. My Kim K. T-shirt and western chaps, but they only pulled out that ensemble when someone needed a laugh—a broken nail, a broken heart, that dreadful episode when Hyacinth discovered that her Eurotrash beau had recently given her the clap. Kowboy Kardashian, they liked to call me. Whoa—Calabasas!

And then I played out my day, climbing through rolls

50 FOOLS FOR LOVE

of felt tacking. Nearly choking to death on loose buttons. (I have had the Heimlich maneuver performed twice—one could get addicted to the high that accompanies autoasphyxiation.) The truth is I generally liked to make a nuisance of myself. I relished getting passed from arms to arms. Being adored.

Sigh.

This heaven was wrenched from me the day I learned to walk. Those of you who have penned your own tales of woe, of avarice and greed, of father- and motherfucking, you sellers and purveyors of sexual deviances in all their splendid peacockian array, those of you who have been kept and those of you who keep, those of you who have been left and those of you who leave, those of you who believe in the public ceremony of opening a vein and bleeding, I am ready to join your numbers.

It's all anyone writes these days. Auto-fucking whatever. Well, this is definitely *my* story to tell!

That is if you don't mind if I bleed for you by proxy. I don't want to spoil my outfit. I will bleed for you on the page.

Indelibly.

It was a Thursday. (Last.)

Grandmama had rung us the night before. No, she said, she would not fork over any more of Dukie's insurance money (in a fit of bratty pique, Buster had spent our last rent check on a Prada moment, this time for herself—bad girl!), but she would happily send a ticket and meet us at the bus station. Home! Some hicksville in East Jesus, Iowa? Where the people shopped at Kmart and I would be the only *bébé-*

BIPOC? NFM. Not for me. Not this puppy. On the other hand, desperate, spendthrift, sex-starved Buster needed time to contemplate her options. So we called in sick, hopping a train uptown.

The playground. Midmorning. Lots of nannies, a stray mom or two stopping by for an air-kiss on their way to Ralph's for coffee, but nothing remotely akin to a dad, eligible or otherwise. Buster deposited me in the sandbox in my sailor suit and went back to her bench to weep. I wasn't about to have any of it. The sand was grody and full of yesterday's drool. Pigeon droppings. A purple fluorescent used condom. "Buster," I yelped. "Maman." But she was too busy with her own woes to care about how I suffered.

In my anger and frustration (justifiable) I reached over for a local fat-boy's pail and shovel. Lucien W. Lucien W. Fat-Boy. He just sat there counting his chins. One, he counted, two, three, four, five, and then he'd start all over again. A fat genius! What a waste he was of Jacadi, squeezed into a handsome blue cashmere cardigan that I had long coveted. You can imagine how appalled I was when lard-ass let one rip. And then he had the audacity to take back his stupid shovel. So, we went at it. Mano a mano. Lucien a Lucien. I confess I kicked his diapered ass.

That is, until the nanny stepped in and smacked me—that Irish wench smacked me!—as I had grabbed Lucien W. by his mousy brown hair, skillfully wrenching it from his lumpy fat-boy skull.

She smacked me. Me, Lucien H. Center of the universe. Il Doge of the playground. King of the babies.

52 FOOLS FOR LOVE

In abject fury, I stood and toddled in the direction of my mother, who hadn't even bothered to turn her pretty head while she and all of North America listened to me wail. Oh, how she wished she was still a virgin back in Iowa, on the dole from her parents, unsullied and slim hipped, still giving all the upstanding local boys wet dreams! Sorry, Ma. I took my first three steps and then tumbled unaided and open-mouthed, ready for disfigurement. *Quelle surprise,* when a *totally* handsome stranger reached down and broke my fall.

"Hey, little man," he said. "Are you all right?"

Was he on drugs? I'd been bullied by a farting fat-boy and physically abused by the same slob's maid. No, indeed, I was not all right and I howled loudly to prove my point.

But this guy didn't bat an eye. "That's okay, bud," he said, rocking me in his well-built arms, arms that didn't feel *too* pumped beneath the cushion of his cashmere. "You'll be just fine."

"Dada," I said.

Why not?

I had been trying out this phrase for months. *Dada, Mama, duck.* One Friday night, when Jack and Buster were numbing their pain over a quart of Wild Turkey, I even said, "Please pass the sauce," but only Jack heard me and he kept it to himself, fearful that Buster might worry that he was hallucinating again and would rethink their babysitting-for-rent arrangement.

I wonder.

Oh Lord, My God, Have Mercy on Me. It's hard to be a baby. Always dependent on the selfish whims and lackluster skills of folks whose calls one might choose to let go straight to voicemail, if only one had the benefit of choice. Picture yourself as an incontinent, penniless paraplegic without language, credit, or a phone of one's own, and only then will you truly remember what it's like to be an infant.

"Dada," I said. At the moment held so squarely and safely aloft, my silken cheek resting against this mystery man's soft shoulder, I wanted to charm as I had been charmed. I wanted him to like me.

"Dada?" repeated Buster, as if in a trance, rising trembly and hopeful from her perch. "Dada?"

Now she heard me.

Buster couldn't believe her eyes: me, cuddled up close to a stranger who looked like money. She opened her arms and for a minute there I thought she wanted to first wrest then toss me, so that he could take her in his embrace, but no, she reached out and cradled me, rocking me against her shoulder.

"Honey bear," she said. "Li'l pup."

What a show. I turned my head and slyly cheesed down her collar. She flinched, but ignored me and my cheese, too busy painting the loveliest of portraits: Madonna and child.

"This little guy was just about to take a fall," my savior said. "I guess he's not that steady on his feet yet."

"He was walking?" asked Buster, batting her baby blues so hard I thought she might take flight. "God, how fast they grow."

They nodded in vapid, attractive, grown-up unison.

"Rob," he said, extending his hand.

54 FOOLS FOR LOVE

Buster looked like she didn't know whether to shake or kiss it. Was she going to lose him? I flashed him a killer grin, thus reeling him back in.

"Your little boy is gorgeous."

Yes.

"Dada," I said, and reached out for him. Once again, Rob took me in his arms. And to cement the deal I planted an open-mouthed kiss on his sculpted jaw. Will you die a thousand deaths if I tell you Mr. Hemsworth returned the favor?

Enraptured, I reached for the hankie in his pocket, thus causing Rob to free up his left hand. *Yes,* I thought. Ringless. No tan line.

"You're a natural at this," said Buster.

"I don't know if I'd call myself a natural," said Rob. "But I'm learning from my daughter. She's just six months old."

Daughter? Warning siren, warning siren. Brrring!

"Isabella spends her mornings in the park."

Isabella? Isabella G. or Q.? A. or zed? Couldn't he have conjured up something a little less obvious?

"Sometimes I come to the park on my lunch hour, just to give her a squeeze, although it looks like the nanny's already taken her home." Here, Rob scanned the playground. "Isabella's mother and I share custody."

Yes! Yes! Yes!

"Would you like to meet her?"

"Oh yes," said Buster.

"Would you, bud?" Rob jostled me.

Do I have to? I flashed Buster, and she flashed back: *If you want to continue to breathe.*

Sure. I beamed him a snaggletoothed grin.

"You're a keeper, bud." Rob burst out laughing. "Why don't the four of us have dinner this evening?"

. . .

You can imagine the hubbub we caused when Buster and I dashed over to the studio. My, how she glowed. The boss didn't even threaten to fire her for calling in sick, on that day or proactively for the next one. Instead, all work stopped as the crew readied us for our date. They freshened her makeup and brushed her hair into long, loose mermaid curls, à la Amanda Seyfried in *Mamma Mia!*—a little retro, but that was part of Buster's midwestern appeal. I was changed out of my sailor suit into Classic Baby Gap jeans and a Molo skate-rat tee, with a Stella McCartney motorcycle jacket—which was fine with me, for I'd been fed lunch during the cab ride from the playground to the studio and my sailor sleeves were slightly yammy. You could take me anywhere in *this* outfit. Then we all sat back and watched the clock tick. Very pre-prom.

At a quarter to six Buster was locked away in the bathroom, artfully pulling wistful strands away from her golden locks so they fell against her cheek and tickled her mouth, begging some someone to gently brush one back, before leaning in to cup her chin, and stealing love's first kiss. I was strategically placed on a little quilt on the floor, ringed by some enchanting vintage toys, a Pooh bear, and a tin truck. Angel and Ira simultaneously kissed my cheeks for good luck—a kiss sandwich!—and excitedly returned to their workstation.

Someone put on some classical music. *Eine Kleine Nacht-*

musik. A little cornball for my tastes, but at least it wasn't too "Here Comes the Bride," aka Pachelbel's Canon. I was glad Buster was occupied. She was a Muzak girl, hatched at Walmart.

At exactly 6:05, they arrived. Rob, extra natty in jeans and an Italian blazer, looking quite fatherly with Isabella tucked safely away in her Snugli.

"Armani," Angel stage-whispered to Ira.

"Classic," Ira kvelled back at him.

"Excuse me," Rob said. "Is Beatrice available?"

"Buster," the boss called, "your chariot has arrived."

"Hey, bud," Rob said when he espied me on the floor. "Do you want to meet my Izzy?"

Sure, I thought. I'll do my part. I flashed him the snaggle-toothed grin he favored, and he unveiled her. Isabella. Out of the Snugli and down on my quilt.

"A-goo," she said. "Alanh."

And even I, King Lucien, couldn't still my beating heart.

For she was lovely. Her hair a crown of golden fuzz. Her eyes blue and brilliant, her mouth a juicy plum. She was dressed in the palest pink. From bootees to lacy bonnet. Making me look far more butch than was necessary, thank you very much. And what ears! Two perfect ivory shells sitting close to her perfect head. Curse that big-lobed, low-life Japanese photographer! (When I'm older I'll have to have mine pinned.)

"Oh," said Buster, emerging from the ladies. "Oh." She herself was as radiant as an angel. "Look at that little doll."

And unfortunately, they all did.

"Ooh," they went. "Aah." The designers and the cutters,

the fit models and Angel and Ira came rushing from all four corners of the studio. They practically knocked me over.

"Baby," they said. To her.

Hello, I said. I'm here.

"Hush," said Buster. "Wait your turn."

Turn? What is "turn"? I began to howl when one of the fit models shoved me aside with her raggedy boot, a faux Isabel Marant Duerto ankle cowboy. I'd told her she wouldn't be happy with a knockoff, but had she listened?

How dare you touch me, I shouted. You Stuart Weitzman–wearing fraud! In contrast, Isabella looked up into the fit model's eyes and gurgled: Appaloosa.

"Isn't she a little princess," said the boss.

Princess? I thought. Fine, let her be a princess. For I am King. King Lucien. King of the babies. King ranks higher than princess any day. Isn't king higher than princess in cards?

But no one in the studio was heeding my declarations.

I know, I thought, I'll pull her hair. Go ahead, cry. But Isabella just looked on me with love.

Bitch, I said. Fight fair.

Whatever do you mean, demurred Isabella, Baby King?

"Look," said Ira. "They're communicating, isn't that completely sweet?"

"I'll spell it out for you, Izzy-boo. T-h-i-n-k y-o-u c-a-n o-p-e-n u-p y-o-u-r e-y-e-s a l-i-t-t-l-e w-i-d-e-r?"

She saucily complied.

"Look at those baby blues," said Buster. "They're as big and round as sunflowers."

Isabella blew her an angel kiss.

58 FOOLS FOR LOVE

"Look, she's blowing kisses, isn't she a darling?"

What about me? I whined. Buster, Maman. I've been blowing kisses for months and months. And to prove my point, I produced an endless supply of iridescent saliva bubbles. But my Buster's attentions had turned elsewhere.

"Rob, do you think that I could hold her?"

"Sure," he said. "Of course."

So Buster took Isabella in her arms and they cooed at each other in mutual blonde bliss. "I'm going to tell you a secret," said Buster, into Isabella's perfect ear. "I always wanted a little girl who looked like me."

And it was true, with their blond hair and their ivory skin, they could have been mother and daughter, while when Buster and I were in the playground we were often confused for some baby pasha and his au pair.

Oh, what can I say, am I proud of the way I behaved? No. But envy, a direct hit, is the fentanyl of the human heart. It left me skittery and nervous, hopped up and out of my mind. I stood and toddled over to the supplies. Did anyone bat an eye? No one in the studio had ever seen me walk before, and still no one bothered to admire me.

"Let's get a picture of Isabella," said the boss, reaching for the camera. "We can hang it on the fridge."

And so it happened that in the few moments it took to get Isabella's frills and flounces and *my* toys to frame her just right, I retrieved the object on which I'd set my eye and toddled back again. Completely unobserved. And just as the boss got that tricky lens to focus, just as he sang out, "Smile pretty, precious," and Isabella cheerily complied, I came up directly behind her.

THE MEMOIRS OF LUCIEN H. **59**

"Look," said Buster, "Lukie wants to be in the picture."
Indeed.

I raised my arm. A flash of silver light. The image caught forever by an iPhone 10. (Fun fact: There is no iPhone 9.)

Now they tell me it hangs blown up on the refrigerator next to the rest of my baby portraits, capturing the moment I went wrong. Me, Lucien H., aiming for Isabella's head with one of the cutters' scissors. I was zeroing in on her soft spot.

Caught in the act. No denying it.

I write this now from jail.

But I'm still a baby, I shout, in the mornings when Buster or Jack drops me off here at day care. Not just any baby, king of the babies, but these days there is no weight behind my bluster, and nobody heeds my calls. It's so unfair, for the scissor's blades barely nicked her, not even warranting a City MD drop-in. Rob, shaken, but still elegant, politely suggested they reschedule dinner for another night. Adults only.

"How about tomorrow?" asked Buster.

God.

Now my days are filled with snot-nosed peasants in Osh-Kosh prison-striped overalls. I am surrounded by subjects, and yet no one here recognizes my magnificence. They are all too busy fighting over their cookies and their blocks, too stupid to know that there are bigger fish to fry. LGBTQ rights! The seasonal shoe sale at Bergdorf's! I have known privilege they don't even have the wherewithal to dream of.

But as day follows day—it has been three since my exile and the commencement of these memoirs, a full week that Rob has yet to call—I am learning more and more to accept my fate. For after our aborted date, when Buster and I returned to our apartment, we stayed up all night, Buster holding me to her breast, her long, silky hair tickling my face, her tears falling fast, mingling with mine. Every so often my beloved would kiss me as she rocked me, passionately, on the lips, the cheeks, my dimpled fists, kisses that both sustained and stung me.

"I hate you," crooned my Buster, "baby, baby, baby. I hate your stupid guts."

Dear reader, was it worth it?

It's okay, I said, hate me. I did what I did for love.

PARENTS' NIGHT

We were at a cocktail party for incoming parents at our daughter's school when I spied my ex-husband amid a sea of ophthalmologic surgeons and hedge fund guys. He was wearing black jeans, a Brioni sports jacket, leather moccasins, and, get this: shades, inside.

How could that be? My ex was a bum.

Mike and I, we'd met in a bar in a Colorado mountain town where, back in the day, the living was still cheap if you lacked standards. (He was cute. I was game and shallow.) We spent most of our time together rock climbing, fighting, having sex, doing drugs, sometimes drunkenly schussing down a snowy mountain, although I hated the cold; both of us, summer and winter, wearing our hair greasy and long beneath filthy knit beanie caps. None of that has anything to do with who I am now—it's ancient history! I'm a divorce attorney. I wear good boots and short skirts. I am married to an arbitrageur of French extraction. Armand. His name sounds like what he is, jewelry you can wear.

Over the years, I forgot about Mike, and sometimes I

thought about him. Now here he was, at an exclusive girls' school on the Upper East Side of Manhattan, milling about near the bar under a banner that said 25 MILLION DOLLAR NEW GYM CHALLENGE! Still good-looking, maybe, but thicker. Like someone had put his handsome face on the copier and pressed Enlarge. What was in my warm white wine?

"Pardon me," I said to my husband, whose silvering head was leaning down toward a rather elegant Japanese woman. They were discussing the cafeteria lunches, which, from what I could glean, needed improvement. No pizza oven. Plus, too much fat. I rested my hand on Armand's arm, the left one, with the circle of diamonds on my fourth finger—Mike and I were so drunk on love we hadn't even bothered with rings. We'd just gotten super stoned and found a justice of the peace and then we'd thrown a party with all our trailertrash barfly pals. After, we went on a camping trip for a honeymoon, and I ate so many shrooms I barfed up my stomach lining.

"Honey. I see an old friend," I said, and my kind, smart, successful husband excused me with an absent-minded smile and a nod.

I walked up to Mike. He had just turned away from a cute little blonde who was apparently his wife. She wore a pink Chanel suit, pink. She was Waspy and thinner and younger than I was.

"Mike," I said.

He looked surprised, but not surprised, to see me.

"Mirra," he said, stopping for a sec. Then, "Baby."

PARENTS' NIGHT **63**

Didn't my stupid knees grow weak.

"What the hell are you doing here?" I asked. It had been about fifteen years, but it could have as easily been a day.

I'd walked out on Mike with a swollen lip, thinking, If I don't get out now, I'll die. I'd assumed he'd gone on to nothing. I'd assumed he'd ended up in rehab somewhere, if he was lucky. Maybe he was dead. Someone said they'd heard he'd gone to Alaska. Alaska, fishing. Maybe he'd drowned.

"Our daughter, Olympia, is entering the first grade," Mike said.

Olympia?

"How can you afford all this, Mike?" I asked. To illustrate my argument, I pointed to the state-of-the-art school auditorium with the Dolby flat-screen liquid-crystal Sensurround whatever that justified the thirty grand we were all shelling out for kindergarten tuition.

"I'm in shipping," said Mike, with a sly little grin. "My wife's brother and I, we're partners. Alaska based. Coco wanted to move back East so that Oly could get the same caliber of education that she had." He sipped his whiskey from a plastic cup. (Some things don't change.) He said "caliber" like he had a hard-on.

"Oly's a Nightingale legacy," said Mike. "Me and my Nightingales."

He was supposed to be the disaster. Now a blonde in pink, a good suit, an Olympia. Two Nightingales.

"You are my husband," I said. I blurted it out. But it was true. He still was my husband. I'd never told anybody in my real life about him, and even though it was my line of work,

64 FOOLS FOR LOVE

I'd never even bothered to divorce him. Call it fear of a busman's holiday. That is, we signed papers, but on no occasion had I had the energy to get up from my desk to actually file them. My secret secret. Which was sort of dangerous, right? A lie like that? It's always been hard for me to stay good for very long.

"I *was* your husband," said Mike. "Then I saved my life."

"I saved *my* life," I said. "You were the one . . . I needed to be rescued from you."

Mike looked at me. His eyes. They were the same kind of fucked-up sick black they'd always been, so dark the pupils melted into the iris, everything melted in those eyes, you kind of got swallowed up and maybe you choked a little. The rest of him was as polished and slightly aged as some prefabricated antique.

"It was us together," said Mike. "The combo was a killer. You were the worst drug of my life." He shook his head slightly. "But wow, was I addicted to you." Then he stared down at his fancy shoes.

Wasn't that the truth? I looked at him now, playing it bashful and vulnerable. Even though I knew it was a game, I experienced such a hungriness, it reminded me of how I'd felt five years ago in London, when Armand had had some business there, and I'd gone along for the ride. We were walking down one of those windy streets in the financial district, no food shops, no restaurants, just banks and office buildings. I was six months pregnant with Lucy. And I was starving. Out of nowhere, that animal ravenousness of pregnancy. When down the street came some poor guy chewing on a roll and

I thought, I'm going to leap on top of you and rip that roll right out of your mouth.

"Introduce me to your wife," I said.

"Okay," said Mike. "But how about we go out on the play roof first and smoke a cigarette?"

"Sure," I said. I was a secret smoker, too. Me and my secrets. Like the cocaine in my lipstick case that I'd scored from the pizza guy on Madison, just in case the reception brought me down. Like the fact that a tour guide had told us the play-terrace door automatically locked at night when a nervous mom asked how they kept the girls safe from custody-case kidnappings when we first visited campus. See, I already knew that once Mike and I were alone and outside that party, we wouldn't be able to get back inside the building.

"Let's go," I said.

"You're on," he said.

There was no turning back, after that.

MY
BEST
FRIEND

I met my best pal, Phil, about ten years ago through our mutual wife. I was a young actor on the rise then, a couple of years out of Juilliard. I'd done two seasons of *Biloxi Blues* (Broadway and a touring company), and although I was raised as a nice Jewish boy, I kept getting cast as a grunt in a series of Oliver Stone flicks because of my Irish tough-guy mug—courtesy of a converted Catholic mother. So the phone was ringing, and the lunches were getting paid for, and the money was pouring in. I mean, I was feeling pretty good about myself back in those days. For a brief while, anyway, I was golden.

At the time, I figured those Vietnam movies were going to be my big break, or actually a series of little ones, running like fractures across a brittle tibia, chipping away at the bone of the business until I was in; but something happened to change all that during my last leg of boot camp in a remote Thai jungle. Oliver had us all go through two weeks of basic training with his own imported drill sergeant; he'd picked the guy up during his much-chronicled tour with the marines. The theory behind all this effort was *verisimilitude,* but it felt more like a frat initiation; he wanted his pretty-boy actors to suffer as much as he had. Me, I went through that whole routine twice—twice a studio flew me first-class to Asia in a Skybed—which back then I thought was pretty cool, but now I see the entire episode as a fulcrum in my life, and if I had my choice of a chapter to reenact from Oliver's nutty autobiography, I'd prefer his early childhood "greed is good" years as the son of a successful New York stockbroker.

See, I sailed through basic training on the first picture like a real Zen warrior—Oliver called me Iron Man, and the rest of the guys looked on me with awe—but what always happens when this dude dares to display a little confidence? I got dysentery: chills, fever, hallucinations, the whole nine yards. And then when *that* was over, I got paranoid. There were all sorts of scary sounds in the underbrush of the jungle, and the vine-covered trees were full of screaming monkeys. I'd taken to constantly looking over my shoulder when I walked back and forth from the trailers to the latrine, brushing the ground before me with a stick. I think I was hunting for land mines.

By the time rehearsals were over and we were into the shoot, I was ten pounds lighter and smoking so much opium I began to believe the set and script were real. I mean I really did. I believed that I was a bona fide member of Charlie Company. I guess that was Oliver's aim. At night, back in the barracks, I had nightmare after nightmare of battle. Bombs blowing up, torched thatched huts, massacres of innocent villagers, skinny dogs. All that Nam-via-Hollywood stuff. Post-traumatic stress by proxy, the doctor on the set

68 FOOLS FOR LOVE

had called it. So much for method acting. But if I do say so myself, it made for one hell of a great performance.

Nevertheless, when I finally got home to New York, all I wanted was a musical here in the city or a rom-com shot in the safety of a lot in Southern California. Jeannie, my best pal Phil's ex and my current, then a casting agent, picked me up at a casting call. She says I had this great romantic, beat-up look back then, she says it seemed like I needed someone to save me, but at the time I think she just wanted out of her marriage, and I was moderately successful and, if I may say so, a pretty sexy guy.

I'm Jake Kaminsky. I grew up as Jake Kamins, son of Dr. Joel Kamins, preeminent ob-gyn on Park Avenue, New York City, New York, a child of the Upper East Side, but when I joined the Screen Actors Guild, there was another Jake Kamins, so I went back to my roots. Took the name of my grandfather, a Russian peasant, one of nine barefoot but scholarly children working a grain mill in a shtetl somewhere in the hard-bitten Latvian fields. Kaminsky. It had a nice European ring to it, and in the early eighties, I thought it lent me a certain air of attractive hunger, a provocative ethnic panache.

Jeannie was scouting for an NBC sitcom, looking for a cop. She called me back three times to read; I performed in a cold, empty studio stripped down to my skivvies. It was a locker-room sequence, broad and humiliating, and she strung me along shamelessly. So I was pretty pissed off, after a month of that tease, when my agent called to tell me I didn't get the part. That is, I was pissed off enough (and intrigued enough) to take matters into my own hands. I marched myself down to Jeannie's office to give her a piece of my mind.

After I'd finished ranting and raving—an impassioned speech about the toll of warfare, Oliver, and the jungle, and how, after all I'd been through for my country, I was entitled to a job—I still didn't get the work, but I certainly got the prize. Jeannie and I went out for beers at the White Horse Tavern, and then I wound up back at her brownstone apartment.

Upstairs, we mixed our liquors as quickly as we could in order to get the particulars on the table and out of the way as soon as possible. Jeannie was at the tail end of a marriage (Phil!) and on her way to Southern California, where she wanted to make it big. She said, "I have impeccable taste." Then she assessed me, professionally speaking, with a practiced eye. She said, "You're a wreck, a hot wreck, which I think should make you increasingly marketable, as soon as you grow out of that dopey GI Joe phase. In fact," she went on, "if my instincts are right—and they're always right—you just *might* become a star!"

It's probably no surprise to you that I didn't.

Jeannie was pretentious and overblown and exceedingly dramatic back then—now she's pretentious and overblown and wound tight—and I liked it, especially the star business; I liked hearing her go on and on about me. But it would be wrong to pretend I actually *listened;* I didn't listen to anything Jeannie said that night, including the married part; I just liked to watch her pace and strut and wiggle around her tiny apartment while I built up the nerve to take her to bed.

At twenty-eight I'd had plenty of experience with women, but that first night spent with Jeannie came after a long psychosis-induced dry spell and it made me nostalgic for the teenage sex I'd never had but had only seen in the movies—high school girls were loath to do it with the son of an ob-gyn, and much of my senior class was made up of my father's patients. By 2:00 a.m. Jeannie had me coming and going in all sorts of directions, and by morning I was so slippery and wet that when she went to hug me naked, I swear I slid a little off the bed. After a shower in the bathroom down the hall, we dressed, me in my same khakis and white shirt, Jeannie in a polka-dot mini and one of those fuzzy sweaters. And then we sat at her little scarred wooden table, and we drank our moldy old orange juice and ate freezer-burned English muffins gazing into each other's eyes.

At around 8:00 a.m., the key turned in the lock, and Phil walked in. Jeannie didn't even bat an eye. "Darling," she said *to me* ("Darling!"), "this is Phil, my husband."

We were fast friends, me and Phil. I mean, we hit it off that morning. I don't know what possessed me to stick around when he first came home, plaid shirt untucked, black jeans stained, biker boots and a soul patch, for God's sake, and a gold band encircling his left ring finger—maybe it was because I already knew that I wanted this girl—but I did stay.

"Hey, darling," said Phil first to me with irony, and then to Jeannie in gentle, sweet defeat.

He was an embattled young novelist, coming home from a night shift as a proofreader at the law firm Sullivan & Cromwell. They had met in a poetry seminar five years earlier at

Bard. "He wrote me love poems," said Jeannie, making a face, a hand over the phone receiver as she called the local deli to see if she could get them to deliver coffee and bagels—we'd given up on the English muffins—which she could. Jeannie could get anyone to deliver anything, except Phil. He was thirty-two years old, he'd gone back to college as an old guy after kicking around for ten years playing bass in a band and waiting tables. "I'm a loser," he said to me, looking for attention. "It's true," said Jeannie. "Ask him what he does all day. Go ahead," my love said cruelly, "ask him what it's like to be a dud."

I nodded in Phil's direction, and Phil confessed, as was his way. In those days he was a beaten man. After the law firm he would usually just strip down to his tighty-whities and lie on the futon couch for a few hours trying to catch a snooze, while Jeannie went to work. Then in the afternoons he'd get up, make spaghetti, and watch crappy reruns. Most of his day was spent, he said, actively not writing his book, not doing much of anything.

So we got to talking, me and Phil, because I liked crappy reruns—visual Valium, I called them—and I liked to read a lot and, let's face it, I'd just poked his wife, so I owed him. We spent the rest of the day together stretched out on the same futon couch, now folded up, that Jeannie and I had spent the better part of the night rolling around on. By the time she came home for dinner, we had moved on to a local bar and back again, and when Jeannie came in the door, we were both already three sheets to the wind and into it—Phil was going to write a screenplay, a star vehicle for me—so we

72 FOOLS FOR LOVE

all ended up arguing plot points and story arcs and ordering Chinese takeout until Phil left for his nine o'clock shift and Jeannie and I unfolded the futon couch again.

. . .

It was only a matter of months of this before Jeannie moved Phil out and me in, only a matter of months after that that she got me to squander the last of my Oliver money on a diamond ring. Phil was my best man. We got married at Phil's mother's country cottage in Connecticut—she was, thank God, away that weekend, or even for us freaks it would have been too weird. And after that, and a honeymoon in Paris (they had gone to Rome), Phil and I still spent most of our weekdays together, meeting for an afternoon movie after a morning audition, sitting in cafés discussing poetry over biscotti and bitter black coffees. He was a good man, Phil. He accepted his defeat easily. He hadn't deserved his wife, and so he'd lost her, period. Most of the time we shot the breeze, we drank or smoked a lot of pot and waxed on and on about our dreams. I was still going to a lot of auditions back then, but I was coming up empty. It took about another two or so years before it became clear that I was permanently unemployed; that my total collapse as an actor, coupled with Jeannie's first pregnancy, made our three-way marriage suddenly untenable. That's when Phil wrote the letter.

Jake, dear Jake,

You're my best friend and all that, but now you've gone and impregnated my wife. There's so much a man can stand. (Ha!

*Ha!) I've decided to borrow some money from my mother
and head out to the beach. Start over, live by the sand and
the sea and do what I was meant to do, be who I was meant
to be. If I can manage to eke out one halfway respectable
novel, even if it's not publishable, I'll figure my time on earth
was well spent. But for now, the two of you are probably
better off without me—I mean maybe now you'll get a job.
(Ha! Ha!)*

Yours in friendship always,
Phil

He left the note hanging on the mirror above my
dresser—he still had his old set of keys. Jeannie was glad
to see him go. "That goddamned good-for-nothing, he's
infected you, you bastard." Not that she didn't believe in
me and my career—some nights when she couldn't sleep,
I'd catch her in the living room watching my reel, trying to
suss out what went wrong—but she was getting hard-edged
and bitter. Impending motherhood, being broke, two wash-
out husbands, it was all too much for her. Little frown lines
played around her eyes.

I did carpentry and urban gardening to avoid them.

Our baby was born in May, two weeks late. We named
her April, because that's what we'd been calling her for nine
months already and we were used to it. Two years later we
had Ethan, her little brother. At this point we had to have a
larger apartment, health benefits, and a babysitter. So I got
a day job. That is, my dad got one for me. I performed high-
resolution sonograms at the neonatal clinic at Mount Sinai

Hospital. All those tiny legs and arms, the baby bracelet of a spine. After the second kid, Jeannie had gone half-time.

We had not heard from Phil since he left town, save for a postcard or two from Mexico that rambled rather awkwardly about the cruelty of poverty and the beauty of the sunsets. Aside from his somewhat-pedestrian letter, these were the only examples I had ever seen of his strained and awkward prose, which resulted in some delicious schadenfreude—I went around the house quoting "the blushing bruise of evening," "the paper-thin quality of money." One horrible winter evening, there was a drunken long-winded phone call when he asked me for a loan, and then begged Jeannie to come back to him. It did sting a bit to hear her say: "Thanks for reminding me that I could be worse off than I am."

After that, shame must have taken hold, because Phil did not even respond to Ethan's birth announcement, and we soon lost track of him altogether, which by that time was fine with me. He had angled for my wife. I didn't miss the guy. In fact, I started associating him with my downfall, a bad influence and all that, contagious lousy karma. I mean, before we'd started hanging out, I'd been riding high.

Sort of.

I was at work one day, reading *People* magazine. Tom Cruise, who I'd worked with on *Born on the Fourth of July,* was on the cover. Johnny Depp and Charlie Sheen (my bunkmates in *Platoon*) were featured on the inside. A girl who had given me a blow job in a closet at a strike-the-set party in Chelsea had just gotten her very own prime-time soap. It was a slow day at the hospital. We'd done four amnios that morning and then nothing. Nothing but coffee from the machine and torn-up, booger-stained magazines. I flipped through the pages with a pencil. Decided to call my agent and was put on hold. I did this from time to time, called in desperation. I held the line and read the story about the actress Dallas Merchant. She was starring in this new show set in the world of fashion magazines, and it was shooting out on the West Coast. (There were no fashion magazines out on the West Coast! In those days they were all on Madison Avenue, but those TV clowns in La-La Land didn't give a shit about *verisimilitude* at all.) She'd been discovered at a giant casting call by the show's producer and creator, Felipe Elbazz, now her fiancé.

Phil. Our Phil! Jeannie's and my mutual husband.

There was an accompanying photo of him, bearded now (all those guys were bearded then—there's a direct correlation, I'm sure of it, between driving ambition and a weakness in the chin), holding hands with Dallas. The caption said he had two other pilots in the can and three more series in development. The happy couple was rebuilding his house in Malibu that just last winter had been hit by a mudslide and fallen into the sea. "A mixed blessing," said Felipe, the producer and creator. "Now there's an excuse to buy all new art and all new furniture, and create the love nest of our dreams."

I wanted to watch him bleed.

For the first time in my life, I understood the saying "jumped out of his skin," for I jumped out of mine. That is, I jumped out of my lab coat. Just jumped out of it, out of my seat, out of my job (for the afternoon). I told the tatted-out receptionist in the lobby that I was coming down with something sniffly—the last thing all those pregnant women wanted was a technician with a cold—and split. And then I walked home, all ninety-nine blocks, to our apartment on First Street and First Avenue. And with every middle-aged step I took, I hated myself a little more.

When I finally arrived, footsore and blistered and halfway out of my mind, Jeannie took one look at me and ran the bath. I'm not ashamed to say that after I stripped down and got naked, after she brought me a beer, I soaked in that hot water and cried my eyes out. She'd never seen me like this, but later on she said it hadn't frightened her. In fact, she said, even a nervous breakdown at that moment felt like a ray of hope.

So when I finished crying, I leaned over and pulled the *People* magazine out of my jacket pocket on the floor. I covered my eyes while my wife read the article sitting on the closed lid of our toilet. Jeannie got up then, I heard her, I felt the breeze of her moving body and the palpable release of tension that came in those days whenever she left a room. And then a moment or two later, Jeannie and all her accompanying anxiety returned—you could sense it rippling across the bathwater. She peeled my hands back with her hands, stuck the cordless phone into my fist.

"Call him," she said. "He owes us."

She added, "I don't care if you have to suck his dick."

And then she sat there and monitored my efforts as, naked and shivering and pitiful, I tried to track down Phil. She sat there as I rang up his mother, *his* office, a string of *his* personal assistants; she sat there as my skin shriveled to the consistency of a prune. And I do believe she was having a rather good time of it, bearing witness, as I prostrated myself to the altar of her ex, for there was a hard, cool light enlivening her eyes and a nasty smile playing around her thin mean lips.

It had been years since I'd made her so happy.

Within three weeks I had quit prenatal at Sinai, and I was safely ensconced in the Hotel Shangri-La in Santa Monica on a modest but adequate per diem. Phil had been delighted to hear from me, "delighted." He'd just written a part into the show *with me in mind,* he said, so we were "fated," and the timing of my phone call couldn't have been more "divine."

I thanked him profusely for his largesse and wondered what it was about LA that made everyone sound like a Gabor sister.

Then I packed my bags.

"Write, don't call," said Jeannie. "Get in the habit of sending child support checks."

Phil instructed his personal assistant to pick me up at the airport in a limo when I arrived, and a basket full of very large fruit—berries the size of quail eggs, a grapefruit that rivaled a melon—was waiting in my hotel room. But it wasn't until the next day on the set that I got a chance to see him. I waited forty-five minutes in his outer office. Finally some D-girl ushered me in. Phil was on the phone, sipping a latte, but he waved me inside with a wide grin, pointing broadly at his cup to see if I wanted my own coffee.

I mimed back no, I was fine, then instantly regretted it.

Even with his face bisected by a phone cord, Phil looked better than I remembered. Gone was that wan, hunched, defeated look that he'd worn like a badge in the eighties. The beard, of course, helped give him definition, but his hair was nicely silvered, and faded jeans hung just so from his slim hips.

Phil's phone call lasted another fifteen minutes. So I awkwardly wandered the office, perused stacks and stacks of scripts, studied his few framed art prints, and then sunk into his couch and stared at my feet. I was still wearing my hospital loafers.

Phil was wearing hand-stitched Italian moccasins.

Finally, he got off the phone.

"Hey, darling," said Phil, walking around the island of his desk to vigorously shake my hand.

"Thanks, Phil," I said, a little too heartfeltly. "I'm really grateful for the opportunity to work."

We both looked away then, I suppose to avoid my further humiliation.

"How's Jeannie?" said Phil.

"Good," I said.

An awkward silence.

Then, "Glad to hear it. And the kids?"

"The kids are fine, Phil."

"Dynamite," said Phil. "Terrific."

Thank God, at that moment, the phone rang, the D-girl barged in, and with a half-blown kiss and another wave of his hand, I was soon shuffled out of Phil's office. After that brief, torturous encounter, I rarely saw my old best friend again. He was always away in Hawaii or Aspen or holed up at his Montana ranch, and the few times he came into the studio, he was breezy and light and avoided yours truly like the plague; which was fine with me. In his absence, it was easier to pretend I had gotten this gig on my own merits.

My part was small, more of an accent, and less than a role, but it was a job, a Guild job, a Guild job with benefits. It had been years since I'd been before a camera, years since I'd been on a set. It had been years since I ate hot Danish and drank cold coffee and stuffed my coat pockets with bagels from the catering table and sat around all day popping peanut M&M's waiting for my three lines. I played Dallas Merchant's ex-husband. I'd come to town as a threat to her present love interest, Chip, a conflicted but good-looking editor at the magazine where she was editor in chief. I started off the season with a series of idle threats. My name was Spencer Klein—another half-breed like myself—and I'd swooped in, ostensibly to buy the company out from under them but really to reclaim Dallas. A cocaine habit on my part had done the marriage in. Dallas was a good girl, if a little overly ambitious, and she favored short, tight suits with slits. Now that I was sober, I wanted a second chance.

Isn't that what I'd prayed for and gotten in my real life? The weeks passed into months. The show shot up in the ratings. Phil, according to Dallas, apparently flew home on weekends, but he was busy running the world then, and except for a couple of quick phone conversations where he was sure to compliment my work—laying it on thick enough to make me feel intellectually challenged—I never really spoke to the guy. Meanwhile, my part grew—Spencer was a real prick, but also, oddly enough, a growing hit with the ladies. I received fan mail. Once with someone's pubic hair in it! He took the network (and Phil) by surprise. So my hours on the set got longer. I'd been away from home for a while, and in some weird way my life in New York began to feel like it belonged to someone else. While I still spoke to the kids on the phone each night, Jeannie was avoiding me. But at the time I felt my career had to be my first priority. If I failed again, the only fallback was going to work for my dad again. So I got more and more caught up in my life in LA. I even rented my own place. And when I closed my eyes at night in my little beach bungalow, when I was driving with the top down and my shades on on the 405, and increasingly when I was rehearsing a scene with Dallas, I was a single guy.

A young single guy. *Under* forty. Trim. Going to the gym. Running on the sand. Drinking Evian water. Receiving fan mail and making money. Massaging Dallas's feet with peppermint foot lotion in the private confines of her trailer.

Spencer was full of dirty tricks. In one episode, while masked and coming up from behind, he'd even pushed Chip out a plate-glass window of a thirty-five-story building. "Thank God," Spencer comforted an innocent and grieving Dallas, "the fountain and pool were there to break his fall." Chip was in a coma, and Dallas and I were in a clinch. On any other show, this would have made a grand season finale, but Phil was a trash-meister of the first element, and he and his team whipped this crap up on a weekly basis. What was shocking was that the worse Spencer got, the more completely he won over the female audience. He was mean, duplicitous, and a hunk of burning love.

"Masterful," a mother of five from Tulsa wrote me. I even got a note from one of my former patients. "I wish I'd known who you were when you were conducting my sonography," she said. And Dallas herself, one afternoon as we were reading lines, said, "You're blowing Chip out of the water, babe."

(The last time she'd called me "babe," as in "You're pulling on my hair, babe," was when we ended up in a closet back at that party in Chelsea, when she was on her knees, and I had one hand on her head, the other clutching at a stand-up vacuum so I wouldn't fall over and ruin the moment. Both of us had opted for selective amnesia regarding that earlier assignation.)

She was a good-looking woman, Dallas. Polished with the blond, gold sheen of a prime-time diva. And she took a healthy pleasure in her own reflection, which, after years of a tight-lipped, frown-lined Jeannie, had its own appeal. While Chip was in a coma, Dallas and I had to do a couple of steamy love scenes. We rehearsed a lot. On and off the set. One evening she even invited me out to their house at the beach. She said, "We've got to crack that damn shower sequence." But before I could drive out on the PCH that night, ready and eager to break my marriage vows, Dallas called me back. Her voice sounded a little shaky. Felipe had just rung her from New York, and after learning of our rehearsal plans, he'd decided to work out of his office in LA. She'd see me Monday on the set.

I took Phil's imminent arrival as a celestial reprieve from

the heinous act I had only moments ago been eager to commit. Jeannie and I may have had our problems then—we always have our problems—but I love the woman. That night I called home, eager to make amends, but the kids were left with a sitter, and Jeannie was out to dinner with a "friend."

"How do I spell your last name again?" asked the sitter.

I hung up, went out, and got so drunk at a popular dive bar in Hollywood that, in the wee hours of the morning, the bartender folded me into a taxi.

Phil had rewritten the next episode. When I arrived on the set, the director took one look, shoved the new script under my arm, and sent me directly into makeup. I learned my latest lines as a cosmetician did her best to "even out my tone," as I was growing paler by the second. Spencer and Dallas were still in the shower, but just when they were about to make use of all that steam, Spencer was to grab his ears and fall down to the floor moaning. A cerebral hemorrhage? Multiple personality disorder? Dallas, naked, would rush out of the water to call an ambulance—the late-night adult audience would be fortunate enough to see her perfect moons. We'd find out what happened to me in the next episode.

And so it went. It seemed that Spencer suffered from post-traumatic stress disorder, thanks to the horror, the horror, of the time he'd spent as a soldier in the jungle—the miniature palm trees and lush bougainvillea in Dallas's solarium triggering his most brutal recollections. Over the next few weeks, Spencer went into a shocking decline. He was reduced to a perspiring, trembling wreck (I wasn't allowed to shave, they oiled my scalp and painted gray streaks around

MY BEST FRIEND **83**

my temples), he was afraid to get off his couch, afraid to do much of anything. And let me tell you, fear like that can be transmittable. For the first time in years, Oliver Stone peopled my dreams. So I was in trouble, but Spencer was worse off. First he lost his business, and then, of course, without money, he lost Dallas. Somehow she'd gotten wind of the fact that he'd thrown Chip out the window—Chip had come out of his coma and was now president of the magazine's parent company—and she'd finally seen Spencer for the bum he was.

I didn't like going to work anymore. My nights were sleepless, lonely, and damp, and I'd show up in the morning totally exhausted. My fan mail morphed into hate mail, and the other actors seemed to avoid me. Even Dallas. I carried the stench of a canceled contract; I could even smell it on myself. Sour, rancid, cheesy. Each Monday morning when the script girl handed me my pages, I took a deep breath and readied myself for my own demise. A suicide, perhaps? A car accident? Dallas and the sexy silver pistol she carried strapped to her left thigh? But there was no easy out for me. Instead, Spencer went back on coke, had hallucinations, lost his apartment, lived in a car, ate out of the garbage pails of fancy restaurants while Dallas and Chip dined royally inside.

I called home and whined to Jeannie. She had been watching the series with apparent glee. The closest she got to sympathy was to say, "I keep telling Phil to either have Spencer buried alive in a coffin or saddled with cement shoes and thrown off the Santa Monica Pier."

"You've talked to Phil?" I said.

"Oh, we've had dinner a couple of times in NYC."

84 FOOLS FOR LOVE

"Honey," I said, "don't you think it's time that you and the kids moved out here?"

"Why?" said my wife. "You're going to be out of a job in another week."

I let this sink in. "Did Phil say something?"

"God," she said. "What a narcissist. We never talk about you." Then Jeannie hung up on me.

That's when I went into my desk and dug out Phil's old letter, which I'd kept as a souvenir. In the past, whenever I felt especially lousy about myself, the letter gave me solace. But now as I read and reread it, it had the opposite effect. The letter was the same old melodramatic mess, overwritten and self-deprecating. "If I can manage to eke out one halfway respectable novel, even if it's not publishable, I'll figure my time on earth was well spent." Phil was practically running an entire network! How could such a loser turn into such a huge success? And on my watch. Off my back. Engaged to my crush. Eating dinner with my wife and actively not discussing me!

I talked to Dallas. That is, I took the opportunity to barge into her trailer. I came bearing that stupid letter, now crumpled and clammy in my fist. I wanted her to see the evidence, to know Phil, the man she was engaged to. A failed novelist. A thirty-five-year-old who'd borrowed money from his mother. A cuckold who befriended the guy who was sleeping with his wife. This is the real Phil, I was going to say with dignity, and here is the written proof. But Dallas allowed me no time for such theatrics. With my mouth barely open, I only got to flap the wrinkled paper before her like a fan.

MY BEST FRIEND **85**

"Poor baby," said Dallas.

The letter took a limp nosedive back into my pocket.

Dallas was sitting at her dressing table in a blue kimono and no makeup, her hair in a ponytail, looking washed out and a little aged. She was reading the next week's script. But before I got a chance to say a word, she gazed up at me with pity. She handed me the pages and said quietly, "I'll go get you a cup of tea." Then Dallas exited her trailer, half dressed, without the comfort of her war paint, onto the bustling set and into the crowded commissary, so I knew in my bones that disaster was probably imminent.

The next episode chilled my blood. According to the script, while freebasing coke—after prostituting myself on Hollywood and Vine to a cruising male pornographer—I had a little accident with the lighter. That is, I was scheduled that Monday to go up in flames, "flames flickering across his face, filling all four corners of the frame" (Phil was a sucker for alliteration). I'd wake up in the hospital with burns over ninety percent of my body. The scene notes suggested that after a week or two of touch-and-go and moan and scream, when no one in the cast would deign to visit me—"What goes around comes around" was Dallas's line, directed to be delivered "tearfully"—I would survive, hideously scarred and completely crippled.

At this point I would come to Chip literally on my hands and knees—the directions said I was to "crawl" up the walkway of his and Dallas's house out at the coastline—and beg for a job as a stock boy at a women's health magazine. Chip, out of the goodness of his heart, was to stroke his beard and agree to hire me if I really could change my ways. A close-up on what used to be my face made it clear that for the life of me, I couldn't. Change, that is. The directions said to focus in on my "evil eyes." "Red streaked and unrepentant." "Surrounded by foamy, blistered skin hanging off in strips."

My hands were shaking. Enough was enough, I was going to confront my maker. I left the set and drove out to the beach.

. . .

When I arrived in Malibu, Phil was sitting at his desk on a deck overhanging a dune with a heart-stopping view of the water. It was a gorgeous day, the air was dry, pressed by the sun into fragrant, soft sheets of breeze. Seagulls lounged about the sky, and the ocean did a cancan across the shore, teasing and retreating, flashing a little ankle. I walked up to the beachside entrance. Phil's head was bent, and as I noted competitively, he still had a full head of hair. The bastard was typing away furiously. Quadriplegia. A colostomy. Penile implants.

It must have been the roar of the waves, or the low, distant rumble of the Pacific Coast Highway, or even perhaps the dynamic state of flow he probably experienced whenever he was destroying me, but Phil did not hear my approach until I was halfway up his stairs. And so, unobserved, I leaned over and picked up a bronze Buddha from a corner shrine Dallas must have purchased to ward off evil and held it behind my back. In the other hand I carried that stupid letter. Thus armed, I continued my ascent, until Phil looked up and rose from his seat.

"Darling," said Phil.

I handed him the letter.

Phil read it slowly, smiling, I figured, when he hit the line about the novel. Then he folded it up and put it in his pocket.

He said, "Do you think I should have it framed?"

That's when I took his Buddha from behind my back and smashed him over the head with it.

I still don't know what possessed me. I was never an aggressive boy, and I'm not a violent man. But that day at the beach, I looked at my wife's ex-husband, a handsome, rich, successful motherfucker, positively glowing in the sunshine on his beachfront property, and I smashed him so hard, blood oozed out and stained his silver head.

For a while it was quiet. Neither of us knew what to do or say. We were shy with each other. Phil slowly brought his hand to his hair, touching blood.

I scuffed the wooden deck with my sneaker.

"I guess I need a towel," said Phil. "And probably some ice." He started into the house, then turned around politely. "You're welcome to come inside."

"No," I said. "I mean, no thanks." I said, "I think I'd better go."

"You're sure?" said Phil.

"Yeah," I said. "I'm sure." And then I said sincerely, "Thanks. Thanks again, Phil, for hiring me."

Phil nodded generously in my direction.

A dribble of blood plopped down on the deck.

"I guess I better tend to this," said Phil, apologetically.

I nodded. And then I turned and started walking toward the staircase.

That's when Phil dived, he literally dived, on top of me, when my back was turned and I was walking away. The whole attack took me by surprise, but of course I should have been ready. He was a stealth bomber, Phil. This was his MO.

We fell against the wood railing of his deck, which sighed and gave, then splintered and crashed, and then like mad wrestlers, we flew off the deck and through the air and down into the dunes. Rolling around, one on top of the other, like tangled pant legs in a dryer, we tumbled onto the shore.

I grabbed a fistful of sand and ground it against Phil's teeth, until something cracked. I pulled back, and he spat a phlegmy, crunchy mess into my face, and then he sunk his molars into my shoulder. I howled and elbowed him so hard, later we found out I'd broken three of his ribs and ruptured his spleen. Phil pummeled my back, bruising my left kidney. Next his elbow fractured my eye socket.

We were trying our damnedest to kill each other.

It was a beautiful day. The sun beat down, but there was just enough wind to keep it cool, so our sweat dried faster than our blood, and our skin stretched taut and cracked as if with paint. As we rolled end over end, sand stuck to our wounds. We were bloody and wet and caked. But as I remember it now, we weren't in pain. Etherized by adrenaline, by competition, by our mutual hate, Phil and I were a tangle of braided muscle rolling toward the sea, so twisted and intertwined we were almost one man.

The water was at low tide, sudsy and blue. It lapped around our edges. And there at the shore, we lay still, so close to each other I could feel Phil's heart beating inside my chest, lending a rhythm to mine; perhaps this alone is what saved me, because when the rescue team finally came and pulled us apart, my heart stopped, and I needed resuscitation.

God, did the tabloids have a field day! And the publicity did wonders for our careers. We sued and countersued each other. And then about a year and a half later, after Jeannie had left and come back to me, after Dallas ran off with her new costar and Phil got a quickie marriage to a very pregnant PA, we called a truce. We met at a bar on the beach, had a couple of beers, and agreed to sell the rights to our story—Phil was to write and to produce, and I was guaranteed a lead. Pay or play. We were once again a team of sorts, although, of course, by then both of us had production companies and families and egos to support, and, true to form, we were each out only for ourselves.

But before, on that glorious day in Malibu, when we were both twisting weakly like a couple of fish on the same hook, it was Phil alone who sustained me. His breath was warm against my neck, his blood salty on my lips, or perhaps it was the brine of the ocean that I tasted, for the waves crashed close and closer still, wetting us now with sea spray. Then it was Phil and me and no one else, and I have to admit I kind of liked it that way, lying half dead in each other's arms when the waves began to break over us, like lovers, curled up in the warm, damp bed of the sand.

P.S.

I t had been a long time between drinks of water for Louise Harrington. It was an early spring outside her office window, and if she craned her neck between the stacks of applications and the stacks of folders that hemmed her windowsill, she could see that beyond her little cubicle the world was full of boys.

Shaggy boys with bandannas leaped through the air like eager golden retrievers to catch a Frisbee with an open jaw of a palm. There were boys without their shirts on. Boys smoking pot and boys flirting and hundreds of boys, it seemed, leaning into hundreds of lank, skinny girls, with lank, skinny hair, in lank, skinny skirts; all these couples hanging out on the great, grand limestone steps of the central library of the university. They were half Louise's age, the boys were, and they all looked like they were getting plenty. What had happened to her life?

She turned to the application in her lap. This particular young man wanted to be a sculptor, he wanted to be a Master of Fine Arts, and he wanted this divine transformation to occur at the very fine institution where she was now acting admissions coordinator. Louise sighed heavily and reached for a cigarette, knocking over another pile of folders with a roughened elbow, an elbow that years ago her ex-husband, Peter, used to massage after her bath with cream. The folders slid to the floor, spilling all those forms covered with sloppy pen and ink that had explicitly stated in bold print: TO BE TYPED ONLY. The floor was a mess. Fighting back the urge to weep, she leaned over, started straightening up. Warshofsky, Evans, Aguado—she'd realphabetize all of them in record time. Louise picked up another folder. Feinstadt, Scott.

Scott fucking Feinstadt.

And for a moment, her heart stopped. It did that now and again, a little mitral-valve-prolapse action, a familiar suspension of her most vital organ, like a dancer's leap, she and her life supports hanging in the air, bridging two moments in time. Then came the crash in her chest, the heavy beating of a desperate bird's wings, the poor thing (her heart) banging up against the sliding glass doors of a patio.

Louise caught her breath. Scott Feinstadt. She petted the outside of his folder.

There had been a Scott Feinstadt when she was a girl growing up in Larchmont. Her Scott Feinstadt had been a painter and a printmaker (a printmaker!), and she'd loved him from afar from the moment she first saw him, which was registration day freshman year of high school. He had a girlfriend then—Scott Feinstadt always had a girlfriend—a beautiful hippie chick, Dallas Merchant, with long, flowing golden hair and long, flowing Indian skirts and toe rings and

92 FOOLS FOR LOVE

earrings and bracelets around her upper arms, one bejeweled job gracing her left ankle—she'd wanted to become an actress and for a while was on a nighttime soap. When the two of them, Scott and Dally, as he called her, walked into the school gym arm in arm that morning, the seas parted, and they skipped to the head of the line, directly in front of Louise. Scott's hair was long then, too. It was thick and black with silver-gray streaks, like a smattering of frost had wafted down and graced it; and it was unbrushed and matted in a long, loose ponytail that was tied with a rubber band.

Three years later, after Dally had been replaced by Trisha the dancer, and Trisha had been replaced by Theresea Lombardi, the dark-eyed daughter of the proprietor of the lone Italian restaurant in Larchmont, and after Theresea had been trifled with and sent back to the kitchen, he was hers. Scott Feinstadt was hers. They dated hot and heavy the summer before her senior year. Scott had just returned home from several months in Italy; his parents and his grandmother had refused to continue writing him advances on his inheritance, so he had come back from Europe to work off his coming art school expenses in a local food emporium called Cheese Bazaar. Louise would wait for him to sweep and close up shop, and then they'd ride around for hours in his beat-up old red truck. He was full of Italian phrases and romantic stories, and she spent hours listening to him while brushing out his long salt-and-pepper locks. They broke up just weeks before he was to drive up to Rhode Island to go to art school. "It's only fair to you," Scott said, one afternoon in the truck, after she had given him a blow job. "I don't want to hold you back; I want you to have a wild and adventurous life." Louise. Wild and adventurous.

It was the drive to Rhode Island that killed him.

He'd never even gotten to school, never got to test his mettle as an artist, never had time to regret his decision, to come to his senses, go crawling back to Louise, to grovel in the dirt. He'd never even had a chance to miss her.

Nor was she granted the booby prize, the status of being his girlfriend at the time of his death. In fact, Scott Feinstadt had just started up a little end-of-summer thing with her best friend, Missy, so Louise had none of the dignity of widowhood, which Missy dined out on for years.

Now she looked down at the folder. Dare she peek inside? Feinstadt, F. Scott.

F. Scott? The name was written in at the top of the application in a tight and even hand. Not typed, of course, but in a rich black ink, perhaps a fountain pen—which her Scott Feinstadt had favored, the wealth and elegance, the gravitas, of oily ink. The letters had nice full curves to them before they feathered away into nothing. She glanced farther down the paragraph. His address was left blank. A post office box. A post office box in Mamaroneck. Mamaroneck, the sister city to her native Larchmont.

She read on. Month and day of birth: August 28. Somehow, it seemed, he'd forgotten to put down the year.

Her Scott Feinstadt (not an F. Scott Feinstadt) had been born on August 28. She knew this because he had also died on August 28—a fact that a lot of people in her town had valued as having some mystical if useless significance but that she had only found creepy and fitting and somehow round: a kid dying the moment he turned nineteen, just as he was becoming a man.

More, there was more. This Scott Feinstadt, F. Scott Feinstadt, was about to graduate from the Rhode Island School of Design. He was a painter and a printmaker. He favored large, oblong canvases, like her Scott Feinstadt had, and he painted only in oils, too, although, unlike her guy, he liked to layer the paint with linseed oil until the colors melted slightly under its weight, "like brown sugar burning," said his essay. He liked to "caramelize" the "hues." F. Scott Feinstadt had also enjoyed a gap year in Italy, where he devoted most of his time to "eating gelati, drinking wine and looking at art, sitting in churches, spending my bar mitzvah money." There was an ironic edge to his essay; it was gently self-mocking but full of self-love as well. "I believe in myself. I guess you could say I believe in myself totally. I want to live wildly and adventurously, which might be interpreted as hubris but is honestly the way I feel about myself."

F. Scott Feinstadt had three recommendation letters, two from the high priest and priestess of RISD and one from Louise's very own high school art teacher, Ms. Cipriani. "While I don't normally approve of high school students painting nudes from living models, Scott's portrait of his girlfriend is reminiscent of one of Matisse's cruder odalisques."

Louise was reeling. Dally, Trisha, Theresea Lombardi, all of his exes, captured in full flower, their finest hour, at the art show of the senior class. It was a town scandal, Rabbi and Mrs. Feinstadt loyally at their son's side, holding their heads high; the girls aflutter, instant celebrities. Her Scott Feinstadt had never immortalized her own naked, nubile image—he'd promised but had never gotten around to it. He'd rather (his words) make love to her than reduce her to a work of art.

She looked down at F. Scott Feinstadt's application. A phone number (401). Without hesitating, she picked up the phone and dialed. The phone rang one time, two times, three; exhausted, she almost rested the receiver in its cradle. But she hung in there. Four rings, five rings, six rings. On the seventh, someone picked up.

"Hey," said a mysterious young man.

"Hey yourself," said Louise.

Why on earth did she say that?

"Boo," he said.

"Boo-hoo," said Louise, nonsensically. "From Columbia School of the Arts admissions."

"So you're not my boo." The young man laughed.

No. Apparently not.

"Is this F. Scott Feinstadt?" she asked, all business.

"Yeah," he said. "Sure." And then, "Louise Harrington from the admissions department, you're not going to believe me, but I was just about to pick up the phone. I forgot to send in my slides. This must be some weird psychic phenomenon, you know?"

"You're telling me," Louise said.

. . .

It was a Wednesday, the day of F. Scott Feinstadt's trumped-up interview. Louise had scheduled him at the end of the day.

This way she could spend the better part of the morning at Emporio Armani trying to find a skirt that looked like one she had bought in the House of Shalimar in 1999. Nineteen ninety-nine. Six years after F. Scott Feinstadt was born. She finally settled on a gauzy eight-tiered swirl that flirted about her ankles. After she paid up—a small down payment on an apartment—Louise slipped into a local coffee shop, made her way into the bathroom, and changed, shoving her jeans into the wastebasket in the corner. She looked at herself hard in the mirror—how rough her skin seemed, how large her pores were—and then took her long brown hair (hair she had blow-dried straight for the first time in seventeen years that morning) out of its clip and fastened it in a silky loose braid. Another look he'd liked.

Back at the office, F. Scott Feinstadt was late by three-quarters of an hour. Louise was prepared for this. He'd always been late before. She'd taken to telling him that the movies started a half hour earlier than they actually began. *The Sixth Sense.* How hard she'd grabbed his right hand during the scene when the kid saw the bloody ghost in the kitchen. So hard, Scott Feinstadt's left hand fell from its working position on her breast.

It was 5:48 exactly. Louise, practically apoplectic, knew this, for she was staring at the clock when F. Scott Feinstadt knocked on her office door, which she'd left an inviting half-way open.

"Hey," he said.

"Hey yourself," said Louise, a little too jovially, before turning around. "Come on in."

She sounded like an admissions officer.

F. Scott Feinstadt came in. Louise swiveled in her chair and sized him up. He was the right height (five feet ten inches), the right weight (one hundred fifty-five). Actually, he looked a little thicker, but he was four years older, four years older than when she'd last laid eyes upon him. His eyes were the same flawed cobalt blue (brown specks). F. Scott Feinstadt wore baggy jeans and a big, striped baggy polo shirt, his dark hair was shaved close to his pretty head, but among the darker patches of his stubble, Louise thought she could see a smattering of silver frost.

So it was him. A little older, perhaps, a little more handily equipped with a set of laugh lines. But it was him. Or some facsimile—a clone, perhaps; a ghost. It was him.

That or his identical nephew.

It was him, now with a tattoo braceleting his wrist, crawling up his arm. When he turned to close the door, she could see a blue-and-green serpent inked across his neck.

It was him, but a variation.

F. Scott Feinstadt was sitting in her office.

God.

Louise began to talk. She appeared to herself to be reciting the entire course catalog in a bureaucratic drone. But inside, inside! *Hey,* she wanted to call out, *it's me, it's me—it's me inside this grown-up body. Under the aerobicized muscles, the thickening skin, under the permanent tan line on my left ring finger, under the scars—inflicted by life, by disappointment, by my weaknesses and jealousies and flaws, inflicted by you!—it's me, it's me, your Sugar Magnolia, your Cinnamon Girl!*

She wanted to crawl across the floor, unzip his pants, and suck on his cock.

Instead she went on and on about the School of the Arts course offerings while she drank him in.

He was slow, flirty, a little shy, asking questions and then answering them himself, as had always been his way.

"I mean, hey, you know, I'm like a rube, raised in the burbs. Providence ain't much of a city. . . . Will I get eaten alive here? I mean, hey, Ms. Louise Harrington, is there any hope in the Big Apple for a small-town loser like me?" He flashed her a killer smile.

"Sure, there's hope," he said, answering himself. He was really smiling now. "There's always hope—right, Louise, you're thinking that there's hope for me. I can tell. I can tell what you're thinking, and it's hopeful. I can read your mind."

. . .

At an outdoor café on upper Broadway, they ate burritos and drank margaritas, letting the sheer force and volume of the begging, amputated homeless drive them inside. And so it was a piece of cake getting him back up to her apartment, with both of them already three sheets to the wind.

Ha. She'd wrangled a beautiful young boy into her home, one she prayed was still in possession of a pair of muscular ridges that rode the knobby track of his spine, of a hairless back, of an abdomen that she remembered came in sections. How long had it been since she'd slept with a body that didn't slide?

How long had it been, honestly, since she'd slept with anyone?

Louise needed this night! So she finagled F. Scott Feinstadt upstairs, pushing away the fear that her own age might prove a deterrent. Somewhere deep in his abnormally young psyche, F. Scott Feinstadt might also remember their other life and miss her nubile image, but then again the Scott Feinstadt that she knew had been less than appreciative of her corporeal gifts. She had been so waiflike and slight back then. It had been hard, when she was dressed, to distinguish her breasts from her ribs. Once, after sex, Scott Feinstadt had insisted on lying on his side on the bed—his penis now a little kickstand—and examining her naked. He had Louise parade back and forth like a model—an embarrassed, awkward, and shy model, with hunched-over shoulders and hands that fluttered about in a weak little fan dance to hide herself. After ten agonizing minutes, Scott declared her pretty okay—which made Louise's head feel light and her cheeks flush hot—if only her butt were a little higher. Then he jumped up from the bed, cupped it in his hands and lifted to prove his point.

Too bad Scott Feinstadt didn't live long enough to fall victim to a slow metabolism, a balding head, and a thickening gut like the rest of the male members of their high school class. Too bad some heartless woman somewhere didn't get to pinch his love handles and giggle when he was striking out as an artist in New York and most needed her support. Too bad someone in as good shape as Louise was right then didn't suggest he take up jogging while, dressed only in socks and a blue-striped button-down and totally vulnerable, he was getting ready to go to work at his uncle's car dealership in New Jersey.

Too bad that, unlike the rest of them, Scott Feinstadt got to die when he was perfect.

But with F. Scott Feinstadt, Louise had the hometown advantage. She knew F. Scott Feinstadt would have a penchant for older women. She remembered Scott Feinstadt telling her this himself when they were lying naked in Manor Park one night seventeen years before on a blanket made up of their cutoffs and black concert T-shirts, her lacy white bra curled like a kitten at his ankles.

It was ex post facto, and over before she knew it, and she was antsy and he was spent, and they were lying a foot apart and not touching on the hot, moist lawn that led up to the little local beach, a tiny pathetic spit of sand—his words punctuated by the obscene wet slap of the sound.

In order to get a conversation going—it was embarrassing, lying apart and naked like that, her thighs squid white in the moonlight; it was embarrassing, to have been as dry as a desert and not to have come and not to have had the time to properly fake it—Louise was bemoaning the fact that she was getting older. A senior. Used goods. When so many pretty skinny little freshman girls were dying to take her place.

She reached out her hand to his.

She didn't want to lose him. No matter how self-centered he was, no matter that he was a lousy lover. She was seventeen. What did she know but lousy lovers? None of that mattered, not the strange pungent mix of his "natural" deodorant and his body odor, his silly affectations, his incredible self-love.

"Not to worry," said Scott Feinstadt. "I really dig older

women. I mean really old, like thirty-four or thirty-five. As long as they're still in shape. Strong girls. That's when they're at their sexual height. For a guy, it's supposed to be around nineteen. So you're lucky. You're catching me at my peak."

Then he rolled over and mounted her again.

But in her apartment, as an adult, making out on her couch with an older but still young F. Scott Feinstadt, Louise changed her tune. I'm lucky, she thought, I'm so very lucky to be here now with him. And it seemed like in the four intervening years—four years F. Scott Feinstadt time—he had picked up some pointers. He was passionate, kissing up and down her neck. He was passionate, worrying at her earlobe. His body was familiar. So boyish and so beautiful. When he pulled his shirt off over the back of his head, his once-hairless chest now sported curly black spirals around the nipples, and farther down, in the bottom quadrants of his stomach, it got curlier and thicker still, leading a woolly path to his groin.

Louise thought, I can't believe how lucky I am. To have a second chance.

"Wait a minute," said F. Scott Feinstadt. "Don't you want to talk?"

Talk?

"You know, get to know each other a little, before, before you and I make love." Here he reached out his hand, took hers in his dry palm.

Make love?

When was the last time anyone had seduced her just by putting her off?

102 FOOLS FOR LOVE

Scott Feinstadt. He'd done the same thing their first time in the back of his truck. He'd gotten her going until she was crazy, and then he'd stopped short, so that Louise was so loose and trembly she felt that if someone were to pull a secret thread she would unravel and fall apart. He'd stopped her, because he was the sensitive one and she the overeager, anxious slut. He'd stopped her, even though he'd done it with Dally and Trisha and Theresea Lombardi and probably half of Rome, while this was Louise's first anything. The experienced Scott Feinstadt had Louise the virgin begging for it.

Now she was older, wiser.

"Okay, F. Scott," she said. "Let's talk."

F. Scott combed his fingers through her fingers. "Your hands are so beautiful—they look like Georgia O'Keeffe's. Are you an artist?"

"No," said Louise. "I'm the School of the Arts acting admissions coordinator."

"I know that, Louise Harrington." He smiled at her shyly. "But what are you in your heart?"

In her heart, that wobbly, faltering muscle, that generator of panic and fear! What was she in her heart but lonely?

"I don't know," said Louise softly. She hated him.

F. Scott Feinstadt's right index finger grazed her collarbone.

"Everyone's an artist in their heart."

She didn't have time for this. But F. Scott Feinstadt was going on. See, his parents were willing to spring for his tuition. He knew he should probably just move out to Williamsburg, get a day job, and paint his ass off, but he'd never really been out of school before, and he guessed—his finger exploring the hollows above her breasts—he was a little scared. Of the real world.

Oh God, thought Louise. I'm not seventeen anymore—I don't have to listen to this.

She decided to take matters into her own hands. Literally.

"Hey, this is all right," F. Scott Feinstadt said.

In a minute, they were both naked and on the floor, existential crises now mercifully forgotten.

He stopped for just a moment to pull his wallet out of his jeans. He plucked out a condom, a fluorescent-yellow lubricated Sheik, and said, "Is this all right? I mean, I wouldn't want you to do anything you didn't want to."

That same old Scott Feinstadt line.

"It's fine," said Louise, "it's good." And when he fumbled a little with the rubber, she said under her breath, "Come on."

Once cloaked, F. Scott Feinstadt stuck out in front of himself like a luminous yellow wand.

He rolled on top of her, so Louise turned the tables this time, and she rolled on top of him. "Mmmm," said F. Scott Feinstadt, "whatever the hell you want."

Who was this guy, this cute young guy, this MFA applicant that Louise was now fucking? Was he really her beloved Scott Feinstadt, her old lost love reincarnate? Or was he just some kid whom she'd practically picked up from the street?

What did it matter, now that she was finally getting a piece of what she wanted? Weren't there always going to be Scott

104 FOOLS FOR LOVE

Feinstadts and F. Scott Feinstadts, a new crop every generation, coming off the sexy-bad-boyfriend assembly line?

Soft boys? Fuck boys?

She'd met more than a few of them since her divorce. Producers, war correspondents, videographers. After thirty they grew their hair long again; they wore it in ponytails. And these guys were always off somewhere, Bali or Morocco or Bhutan, and they were always hopelessly in love with some Peace Corps gal or an Iranian photographer or, if they were white, a gorgeous mixed-race actress who just got cast in an upscale miniseries; some woman who jerked and jerked and jerked them around, who jerked them around so much they couldn't help jerking you around, too, these Scott and F. Scott Feinstadts. It was the trickle-down theory of romance.

But now Louise was on top. She was on top and liking it. This F. Scott Feinstadt had melted into a blissful and helpless puddle between her hips. Every few seconds, he would arch up or thrust or twitch or something, a little weak smile teasing at his lips, but at best his rhythm was syncopated and close to annoying; so, soon, through caresses and a careful squeezing of her inner organs, Louise seized control of the situation, F. Scott Feinstadt giving up.

When they were young, Louise and Scott Feinstadt, the summer nights in Larchmont were thick with the scent of pollen and perfume, the smell of gasoline, of pot, of cigarettes, of bug spray and his deodorant. Their fledgling naked bodies were softened by the filmy haze of suburban starlight; they were as blurry and unreal as if a cinematographer were viewing them through a layer of shimmery gauze. When they were young, Louise would spread her legs and let Scott Feinstadt enter her, whether she was ready or not, whether it hurt her or not, and she'd say, "I love you, Scott, I love you, honey," in intervals of about seventy-five seconds. She counted. She counted the intervals between her words of encouragement and the moments until it was over. Sometimes, sometimes, it felt like his fucking her went on forever; then other times it was over before she knew it.

But when it was over, when he had come, when he had finished, he would completely collapse, sinking down on Louise, his hip bone grinding into her pelvis; the weight of his body flattening out her lungs, making it hard to breathe; the soft, tender tissue of her vagina aflame and burning—so much so that after a couple of rounds of this, when she peed later, even in the shower, it would sting. And she'd think, Someday I will find someone who loves me; someday I'll get married and have a husband; someday sex will be something I like, I love—it will be something good.

Now, in her apartment with F. Scott Feinstadt, it was Louise who was keeping it going, getting him to the brink, then pulling back, then getting him to the brink again. The poor kid was all shiver and moan.

"Oh God," he said, "thank you. Thank you, God, a lot."

With a slow in and out she pleased him.

Only when he gave up the ghost did she finally allow herself to come. And then they slid away from each other in a loose knot, on her living room floor, F. Scott Feinstadt's right arm slung haphazardly across her waist as he lightly, lightly began to snore, while Louise tried to even out her own breathing, to calm her racing heart.

Now she was lying half clothed—for she still had her T-shirt on—on her floor with a boy half her age, dead asleep, in her arms, with a boy she didn't know. His mouth was open, and a little spit bubble breathed in and out of the corner. She smelled his buzzed head; it was as sweaty and sweet as a baby's. What had she done? She could lose her job for this. Now that he'd slept with her, maybe this strange kid thought he could gain admission to the graduate program of his choice. Or worse yet, he just might fall in love.

She wriggled out from under his arm. She covered him with one of her sofa throws. Then she got up and went into the kitchen, looking for a cigarette. In the cookie jar was her emergency pack. She tapped one out and lit up. Smoking, she went back into the living room. A beautiful naked boy was sleeping on her rug.

She'd fucked him.

When they were young, when they were done, Louise would trace the words *I love you* across Scott Feinstadt's still-panting moist back with the tip of her right forefinger—employing the same hope and delicacy with which she might have traced those heartfelt words on a steamed-up back-seat window. And she'd say, "That was great, Scott—I really love you," which was true. The second part was true: She really did; she really did love him. She loved him and she loved him and she loved him, and she was never going to get over him, no matter what anybody had to say about puppy love and life experience. No, Louise never was going to get over the stupid dead boy she loved with all her heart when she was so ridiculously, improbably young that it should have been against the law.

It should have been against the law back then to have been as young as Louise Harrington once was.

And now, at last, she's old.

THE
INTERVIEW

How the hell do they interview a child who cannot speak?

It was the start of twinset season, and Mirra, that shameless impostor, was carefully donning the creamy sleeveless cashmere cap-sleeved scoop neck and cardigan that she had stuffed away so victoriously when she'd twice hit the bell with her two older daughters, so many years before. Fat envelopes of acceptance. Fat tuition bills. Mirra peered at herself in her bedroom mirror. She looked ropy and European; like her body was younger than her skin. Her brown hair was blown back into a glossy ponytail. She added lipstick and earrings to complete the artifice.

Of course, both her daughters had aced their way into appropriate girls' schools—brainy Lucy at the challenging, refined Nightingale and popular fun-loving Charlotte at the fizzier, partying Spence—they'd proved superior from the get-go. They had her former husband's brilliant genes. Armand was still an arbitrageur, dividing his time now between Paris and his third wife and a pied-à-terre in the Village, where each daughter had her own room as part of their visitation agreement. Mirra's latest husband, Dr. Dan, her second and a half (long story), the father of her little guy, was no dummy either. He was a Jew and a neurosurgeon, she'd decided to finally make someone happy—her mother—and he was always flying off here or there to operate on some famous actor or world leader or the sultan of Brunei; it seemed to Mirra that Dan was always operating on the sultan of Brunei. She sighed. In the mirror her face was older, and, when she flipped around, her butt flatter, than she felt inside. All that dieting. She unbuttoned the top three buttons of her cardigan to display her collarbones, because she'd earned them.

Both her girls had been talking since the age they could walk. Not little Adam. Adam was her anchor baby; she'd been a matrimonial attorney when she and Armand split up. (She'd dived headfirst into a doomed, tawdry, back-to-the-future affair with her still-a-drug-addict starter husband; word of warning, don't ever do that!) Thank God Armand was French, so after the fireworks died down, none of it turned out *that* ugly. Mirra knew from ugly, it was how she'd met Dr. Dan; he'd been one of her clients. Dr. Dan had wanted his own progeny. By the time they'd hooked up, Mirra was sick of working anyway, and an infant gave her an open-ended leave of absence.

Adam, with his golden curls and creamy coffee-colored eyes, with his snotty nose and sturdy little body, his sporadic outbursts, the dark storm of his temper tantrums, the whirl of his legs, the power of his baby punches, his thighs as cut and defined as that actor Milo Ventimiglia's, was the child of Mirra's heart, but he was not a talker.

Adam could push both of his big sisters in a shopping

cart through the crowded aisles of Food Emporium. Adam could, in the midst of one of his terrible-three-plus explosions, require both herself and Ofelia, the most recent in a string of reluctant babysitters, to quiet his flailing arms and fold him into a stroller to ferry him safely home. Ofelia was French, too, French North African, raised in Paris, all of this had pleased Armand, who wanted to keep his daughters bilingual. Dr. Dan couldn't give a shit one way or the other. Fine with her.

Adam could shout and laugh and cry with the best of them. But aside from the words *mama* and *mine,* the kid was mute. This hadn't exactly worried Mirra much before she had to face a brand-new round of nursery school interviews; in fact, before this newest twinset season, her son's lack of language had been a source of comfort.

Mirra liked the fact that she and Adam communicated silently. Physically. Through slippery kisses and big bear hugs. Those girls were such chatterboxes. Often Mirra found herself standing behind one of them as the kid in question prattled on and on about the portraits of Joseph Roulin— Joseph Roulin? "Van Gogh's postman, Mom!"—or when one joined the other doing some dopey new boy-band song-and-dance routine, with Mirra silently mouthing the words *Shut the fuck up* behind their twerking bottoms.

Adam was her confidant. When they were home alone she did not even have to whisper. Adam would be building a tower of blocks, and Mirra would say: "Daddy's so fat, all those rolls around his belly. I can barely find his penis," and "One day I'm going to pack our bags and you and I are going to head back out West, to Colorado," stuff like that, stuff that she would never ever dare tell someone who was capable of repeating it. Mirra liked the fact that after she finished with whatever tirade seemed to spew out of her mouth, Adam would stare at her googly-eyed, press his goobery cheek to hers, and then ignore her. She liked the fact that he still took a bottle and a pacifier, she liked that he could stuff both simultaneously between his lips and that when he did the house was completely noiseless except for the sound of their breathing. She liked when they breathed in sync, effortlessly, yogicly, when they were one.

Night after night, after the girls had gone to bed when Dan was working late, operating on someone's brain—for God's sake, the hubris! the Dan-ness!—Adam would fall asleep in her arms, his sweaty little curls pressed against her bony clavicle. Mirra liked more than anything that he was still a baby. She could kiss him anywhere on his body—his tummy, his chest, his tush—whenever she wanted. The luxury of it all.

In the kitchen, Ofelia, in her white jeans and matching tank top, braless, was feeding Adam a banana, earbuds in her ears, startlingly bright against her smooth dark brown skin. They looked like one of those old Benetton commercials. She was stunning, Ofelia, six feet tall, all of it legs. How cute Adam was in her arms, cramming the soft fleshy fruit into his rounded cheeks. He was all gussied up, too: blue cords and a big-boy button-down shirt. Ofelia had brushed his hair so that it lay slick and wet across his forehead, but still his curls were already springing back into action.

112 FOOLS FOR LOVE

"O," Mirra said, "could you please pick up Charlotte and take her to ballet? Today is the day of Adam's school interview."

Ofelia nodded; no one had been allowed to forget this hallowed date. Mirra had been stressing about it all summer. But at this exact moment, Adam was a lamb. Mirra had learned the hard way that as long as she asked Adam for permission first, with a little luck, she could mostly get him to do as she pleased.

"Sweetie," she said, "can we put on our jackie now?" He allowed his chubby little arms to be pulled through the sleeves of his miniature blue blazer; he gurgled and smiled as Mirra buttoned him up. It was a Tuesday. Tuesday mornings he often accompanied Mirra on her secret missions. Tuesday mornings for Adam were Mommy time. He walked out of the apartment without a fuss, Ofelia closing the door behind them with a thunk. Mirra would never ask, but she hoped that with Adam out of her hair, Ofelia would make some inroads into the mountain of clean laundry strewn suggestively on the living room sofa.

Out in the crisp fall air, Mirra asked Adam to hail her a taxi. This he was good at. Why, if the interviewer could see him now, his determined little expression, his hand shooting up into the air so authoritatively, she would recognize his superiority, take note of the fact that this child had management capabilities, he could lead. Mirra should have put this specific skill down on his application. After all, the various admission forms had included a space for "your child's special interests and talents." What were Adam's? Applied physics? Avant-garde theater? He was terrific at knocking a tower of blocks over—so Mirra had marveled in her essay about his gross-motor capabilities. He was proficient at scribbling across Lucy's precious paintings with indelible Magic Marker, so she'd rhapsodized about his love of art. When the theme song for *Sesame Street* began to warble through the apartment at the end of the day when Mirra was already deep in the bottle and ready to tear her hair out—she'd buy cases of Beaujolais nouveau, the cheap stuff, and drink it past its prime—little Adam would come running to the TV like a homing pigeon. So she'd emphasized his passion for music, its ability to both delight and calm him. But Mirra had forgotten to mention his expertise at hailing a cab. Spatial relationships, physical prowess, confidence, confidence, confidence.

Now, her gifted, commanding, potent son deftly waved down a taxi. They climbed in without a fuss, although during this ride, like all the others, she had her heart in her throat, because he refused to sit in her lap. He refused to sit period. Mirra couldn't just slip the seat belt around him the way she'd always done with his compliant sisters. Instead Adam rolled around, pushing buttons, the window, good God, the locks, forcing the little Plexiglas change slot back and forth so that the scratchy sound would drive anyone in earshot nuts.

Mirra apologized over and over again to the driver, saying, "Adam, please sit, Adam, please—baby danger," just so the cabbie wouldn't think she was a disaster as a mother, when really all she wanted to do was look out the window and space out, daydreaming a tragic accident in which both

114 FOOLS FOR LOVE

mother and son could escape from this messy, clamorous world together. By the time the cab pulled up in front of the apartment building of her lover, both Mirra and Adam were in a sweat, she could feel her underarms staining that damned sweater set, and Adam had a little pearly string of moist beads gracing his upper lip and brow. She wiped it away with a pursed mouth. Mirra tipped the cabbie a couple of extra dollars and hightailed it out of there, afraid as always to turn into Lot's wife, to look back.

Joshua, Mirra's boy on the side, was Charlotte's English teacher. Mirra had met him first at a parent-teacher conference and then, after some strategic volunteering, she had virtually thrown herself at him at a series of book-fair meetings. Mirra had always been willing. In high school, in college—thank God she'd grown up at a time when lunatic sexual behavior was expected; she'd been able to have her cake and eat it whenever she wanted without any damage to her reputation. In truth, her desirous nature had been one of the things that helped her rope in this husband—Dan's first wife had been more of a once-a-monther. Now, since Dan's interest had waned to what felt like vacations and birthdays, her fulsome and needy sexuality had become a liability.

Mirra had seen this transgression—throwing herself at the younger, vulnerable Joshua—as an act of self-preservation. She flirted and flirted until the poor guy had had no choice but to ask her out. She would never forget it, Joshua's shambling shy and bookish manner, the way he wouldn't meet her eye when he said, "Mrs. Eichler?" Mrs. Eichler! "I could use your advice, uh, around . . . book ordering? Perhaps we could

THE INTERVIEW **115**

have a cup of coffee?" He was as young and smart and nerdy and sweet as she liked to pretend Dan must have been in his prime.

A cup of coffee indeed. Right then, Mirra had known that sometime in the immediate future Joshua would be left standing and she'd be on her knees, and she'd wondered to herself if, when he came, a gorgeous and enlightening string of poetry would ejaculate from his mouth. But first a proper courtship had to ensue. There was no cut to the chase with matters this delicate. She was in her forties, she'd had enough experience to know not to rush things, when all she ever wanted to do was rush things. She wanted to rush Joshua right into her bed, his face between her thighs, her hands in his hair, the bedroom air moist and fertile as a rainforest, her favorite TV show on in the background. But with age comes wisdom, restraint; this she told Adam as she stirred his oatmeal one morning, after the girls had gone to school and Dan had strutted off to the office, when she was plotting about Joshua and doing the breakfast dishes and fixing Adam a healthy snack all at the same time—multitasking. Wisdom, restraint. Growing old.

So Mirra had agreed to join Joshua's committee of two. They'd meet in a neighborhood coffee shop, Adam methodically emptying all the sugar sachets, the salt and pepper shakers, the little individually packaged jams and honeys, the ketchup and mustard packets, into some weird cosmic soup onto the table, while Mirra and Joshua put their heads together over the book orders.

How many Eric Carle? How many Dr. Seuss? Joshua's

116 FOOLS FOR LOVE

hair was black and curly, with a pattern of graying threads bejeweling his well-stocked head. He reminded Mirra of a rabbi, his gentle searching manner, his tender avuncular humor, the wisdom of his anecdotes, that little yarmulke of a bald spot. He was cute. And bespectacled in a cool, intellectual way—silver frames perched lightly on his nose. Even through that thick glass his eyes were an iridescent, mesmerizing hazel. With the wafting odor of fry fat perfuming their hair, the coffee that looked and tasted like melted-brown-crayon water, the soggy BLTs wilting on the chipped china plates that squatted on chintzy paper place mats, Mirra and Joshua would press their knees together under the table in the corner booth—Adam under the table with his toy cars to document this—until the day they graduated to Joshua's apartment.

Every Tuesday morning, while Joshua with his PhD from Princeton, his MA from Yale, his BA from Columbia (all Ivy, Mirra noted with pride) was home doing "course prep"—Charlotte's school was famous for "course prep," for instructor sabbaticals and all-expense-paid trips to Europe for further study—while Joshua the academic was preparing to teach the privileged and the gifted, and his artist wife, Shoshanna, the heiress to a fortune amassed from the manufacturing of labels for designer underwear, worked at her studio out in Long Island City, Adam and Mirra paid their weekly visit. Mirra and Joshua would fuck in the maid's room, with the door open and the little portable TV turned on to some dumb cowboy game show, the "hee-haws" drowning out the escalating arpeggios of their moans, while Adam busied himself in the kitchen, pulling the pots and pans out of the cabinets. From the clanging sounds of the crashing metal, Mirra could assure herself that Adam was still living and unharmed.

Today's visit was not a sex visit. Too bad. Sex would be great on a day like today, interview day, a day when she was anxious. But sex had to be put on hold for a while. Joshua met them eagerly at the door. He put his hand out for a high-five, but Adam would have none of it. That little homing pigeon Adam headed straight for the kitchen.

"I am so very glad you've come," said Joshua to Mirra, and he looked glad, he looked desperate, he looked sweaty and shaky and, well, unattractive. He looked a little like a grad student. He had recently been caught embezzling book-fair funds by one of the more dastardly administrators at the school, a coldhearted spinster alumna of the very same institution. He'd been trying to collect enough money to escape, so that he could get out from under the economic thumb of the wife who neither respected nor coveted him. Mirra understood his situation. So although Mirra had been privy to his ridiculous plan, she hadn't bothered to stop him. If he hung his own rope, she'd have a graceful exit strategy. And actually, she'd been a little flattered, because Joshua had made noises about her and Adam accompanying him. Fat chance, she'd told Adam.

Joshua took her hand. His palm was damp. "Yuck," said Mirra. Of course, Joshua was miserable; he faced certain termination, perhaps an indictment or, worst of all, a nose-holding acquiescence to the wretched and desperate administrator's sexual advances, but did he have to wear his misery so obviously? Here's where an icy narcissistic self-confidence like Dan's took on a certain luster. Far preferable to this wilting lettuce leaf of a man. She shook herself loose and followed her son into the kitchen.

"Would you like a cup of tea?" asked Joshua, trailing after her. "We are in possession of a particularly interesting leaf, termed, appropriately enough, gunpowder. Perhaps I could use it to off myself. Shoshanna brought it back from her pilgrimage to India."

"Constant Comment," said Mirra. She sat down at the undersized round table, the sunshine spilling inexplicably through the air shaft and warming a little square of the butcher block where she rested her arms and waited for him to serve her. (It reminded her of her parents' kitchen, that pizza-box cube of light.) Another reason she was fond of Joshua, besides the fact that he was smart and actually liked to go down on her, was that he did indeed serve her. At this point in her life no one ever served her, unless you counted the knowing, smirking waitress in the coffee shop. At this point in her life Mirra served everyone around her—*Mommy, juice please; Sweetie, drop off the dry cleaning?*—everyone except him. Too bad Joshua was such a failure. As an academic, as a husband, as a thief. But as criminals went, wasn't he the best kind? Taking from the rich to give to the poor, stealing from her and her overprivileged children? Mirra felt dizzy with confusion, as if she were tumbling down a long tunnel, internal compass, as always, failing her.

"You look so beautiful in that light," said Joshua. "You look like a Sargent, in that sweater you look moneyed and elegant like a Sargent. You look lit from within like a Vermeer."

What was this, a tour through the Metropolitan Museum of Art? Still, Mirra was flattered. She knew she was not beautiful, but it was kind of him to think so, kinder still to lie to her about it, because a lie took so much more effort than the truth.

"Today is Adam's interview," said Mirra, by way of explanation.

Joshua nodded an "of course" nod. He remembered. This fact made her like him again. Her concerns were his concerns. He was practiced in the art of empathy. As if he could sense this, her subtle shift, Joshua sank to his knees by her side and placed his head in her lap.

How pink and shiny was his bald spot. Mirra petted his hair anyway around the exposed, pathetic skin with one hand, and with the other she dug deep into her pocket.

She and Adam had gone to the bank that very morning, before Ofelia had arrived and after dropping the girls off at the bus stop. She and Adam had written a check out of her cousin Teddy's account made out to cash. Mirra managed his finances, Teddy's. Mirra the attorney had power of attorney. Teddy had been run over by a car or a truck or a human mob in jerkwater Idaho, three years ago, where he had been dealing drugs and guns, or maybe was just not working? It was also possible he'd fallen from an overpass or out of a tree? Mirra hadn't known what hit him, and neither, she suspected, had her cousin, because the alcohol level in his blood was three times the legal limit, and that didn't even count the pharmaceuticals. He was found by the side of the road, in the a.m., about a hundred yards beyond a local bar where he'd been seen drinking the night before by various ruffians of dubious reliability.

Since his parents were both dead, her parents too old, and her other two siblings, a sister and a brother, lived in London and LA, respectively, and she was a "money person," Teddy was her charge—for which she was paid a small monthly salary. She set him up in a nursing home on upper Fifth Avenue. He could neither speak nor eat; he was fed through a tube in his belly. No one knew if he could hear or perceive or register; he was riddled with bedsores that burrowed from his skin down to the bone. And he hadn't exactly been great shakes when he was still animated. As a child he'd been a cruel, vicious bully. As an adolescent, a delinquent and an addict. As an adult he'd been a lowlife, two-bit gambler. Still, he was Mirra's charge.

She'd reluctantly supervised his medical treatment, visited him with Adam once a month, handled his finances and his inheritance. But this was the first time that she'd stolen from him. She and Adam had withdrawn five thousand dollars, enough to cover the embezzlement, to get Joshua off her back. Hush money. Joshua could see it as a loan, or whatever. He could pay back what he owed and then some. He could take off. Do with it what he desired. As long as he effectively disappeared. It had all gotten a little too complicated.

Three weeks ago, Joshua had said, "I love you, Mirra."

Mirra had felt dizzy with regret when he'd said it. His love was not the love she wanted. And when Mirra looked up and away from Joshua's beseeching gaze, she could have sworn she saw Adam roll his eyes and make a cutting motion with a finger at his throat.

Now Adam stopped his pot stacking and his crashing. His big brown eyes locked on his mother. He gave her a subtle nod. Together they had planned this moment.

"Joshua," said Mirra.

He looked up. He was still on his knees.

She reached into her pocket, pulled out the check, handed him the dough.

It took Joshua a moment to make sense of the thing. Then he began to smile.

"So you guys will come with me?" asked Joshua, half as a question, half as a statement. He said it with stupid hope.

Adam shot her a look.

"No," said Mirra. "It's for you." She winked over his head at her son.

"Without you, I don't want it," said Joshua.

"Sure you do," said Mirra. "Without it you could go to jail."

For a moment the room was silent.

"I'll pay you back," said Joshua, looking at the floor. There was some spaghetti sauce splashed on the grout between the tiles. He worked at it with his thumbnail.

"Of course you will," said Mirra.

. . .

Outside, in the soft, warm early autumn sunshine, Mirra looked at her watch. There was still enough time to take

Adam to see her cousin. As the years had passed, her visits had become shorter and shorter. Her own mother used to come with her sometimes, too, although now Lily found it too upsetting. She was a more delicate creature than her daughter, apparently.

Teddy had grown so thin; his muscles had atrophied, and not only his hands and feet but his arms and legs had clawed. Adam was a welcome menace around the breathing and feeding tubes, the IV and the catheter—chasing after him in Teddy's room had kept her busy; and she'd won points with the nursing home staff by bringing her little boy along.

"What a devoted cousin," the health-care attendants said when they made their monthly trip. The health-care attendants did not know that Mirra whispered in her cousin's ears: "You got what you deserved." Only Adam knew. Only Adam knew how much she reviled the cousin who during his teenage years had forced her head between his legs, who had beaten her for sport as a child when he was asked to "baby-sit" her.

Where were her out-to-lunch activist parents and aunt and uncle then? At some Michael Dukakis fundraiser? Opening a New York chapter of Peace Now? She hated these visits, but she liked them, too. She liked that Teddy was in a position where he could no longer harm her.

Joshua lived in Teddy's neighborhood. There was enough time to run over there, make nice to the nurses, earn her medal of honor, and then whisper into her cousin's ear that living well was the best revenge, so she was now officially stealing money from him. There would have been some new

THE INTERVIEW **123**

form of grim satisfaction in all that. But then again, she and Adam could go get a cookie and a coffee before walking over to the school.

Mirra strolled down Madison Avenue with her little boy's hand in hers. They stopped in at one of those faux-Parisian fancy food shops. Mirra bought a cupcake for Adam and one for herself—they'd earned this little repast—and a cappuccino to fortify her. He ate quietly and diligently as they watched the traffic from the store's ceiling-to-floor plate glass. So many mothers with their children. So many well-dressed mothers with their well-dressed children. Mothers with ponytails like hers, mothers with manicures like hers, with good shoes and good bags, mothers with custodianship of designer cashmere twinsets. If Mirra scratched their surfaces, would they all be in possession of secret lives as hideous and knotty as hers was? Or would she just end up with a fingernail full of one-hundred-and-eighty-dollar face cream?

When the Muffy mommies glanced in the food shop's window, when they saw Mirra and her little Adam, gorgeous and calm and eating a cupcake, were they envious of the tableau? Did they truly believe she was one of them?

Mirra brought her cappuccino to her lips, but somehow a tiny bit of milky coffee dribbled out of her mouth, landing on the creamy perfection of her cap-sleeved scoop neck. Shit. She dabbed at the blot with a napkin that she dipped into Adam's plastic cup of water. Too bad some of the sprinkles from his cupcake had already fallen in. Her sweater was now marred with a small rainbow-colored blemish. The more she worked it, the more the rainbow began to spread, the colors continuing to bleed. It was too much. In the frame of the plate-glass window Mirra began to weep.

With all those people watching, Mirra wept, silently and wetly, mascara running down her cheeks. Adam was the only one who tried to comfort her. He placed his little chocolaty cheek on her good wool slacks. It was a sartorial disaster. In the lexicon of independent schools, dishevelment was a deal-breaker. But without entry into the proper preschool, one could not hope for a first-tier ongoing school. Without a first-tier ongoing school, what would be his prospects for a highly ranked college? More than anything, Mirra wanted this child to have a good life.

. . .

After a quick trip to the ladies' room in the Hotel Wales across the street, Adam's face was scrubbed, Mirra's face was scrubbed, and the cardigan of her sweater set was buttoned closed into one smooth long schoolmarmy line, conservative and smart, appropriate once again for the task at hand. As she studied herself in the mirror, Mirra's racing heart went back to normal. She could do this, she told herself. She could pull it off. A swift glance at the lobby clock informed her that they were ten minutes away from liftoff. She picked up Adam in an effort to run him across the street to the school. Dan would be outside the building, wondering where they were. He'd be tapping his foot in annoyance. He never waited for anyone. People waited for him. Dan was a neurosurgeon. At times like this, Mirra was sure, he would happily rearrange her brain if he could get away with it.

But picking up Adam was Mirra's great mistake, her fatal one, in a day that had been so thoughtfully and still—how did this happen?—so recklessly calibrated. She'd picked Adam up without asking his permission first. She'd lost her head. Forgotten protocol. She'd neglected to say, "Sweet boy, can Mama go uppie?" As soon as she lifted his little body into the air, she realized her error in judgment, for his calm, peachy-skinned, clean, and shining face instantly turned purple, his little legs began to bicycle, his arms began to windmill, his body to torque and arch. And then, after a moment of delay, as with a sonic boom, came the ear-shattering screams. "Please, baby, please," said Mirra as she struggled to hustle him out of the lobby. "Please, my love, not now." Time was running out.

When she reached the sidewalk, Adam was going full throttle; she could barely hold on to him. He hit her in the face, the neck, his feet kicking at her stomach, her legs, her knees; after a particularly good wallop, she almost dropped him, and his strong little body sagged perilously close to the ground.

Fortunately, Dan was waiting on the opposite corner, looking at his watch. Dan was short and unfit and wearing the blue suit she'd laid out for him that morning. His cheeks were tan; he'd just returned from some surgical conference in Palm Beach. Somehow, through aging and accomplishments, he'd become a formidable, coldhearted, portly man. Why didn't he care enough now to glance across the traffic, see Mirra's predicament, and rescue her? She tried to scream for help, but Adam's cries were far louder than hers. It must have been this familiar sound, the bloodcurdling shrieks, that forced Dan to look up and notice them. When the light changed, he slowly crossed the street, disgust plastered across his face.

"What now?" said Dan by way of greeting. "We're late enough as it is."

"This wasn't exactly my idea," Mirra hissed at him.

A mother from Charlotte's school was getting out of a taxi. Mirra didn't want her to see them. She turned her back, which set Adam's wails to a higher frequency.

"Adam, you must quiet down," said Dan, with a distanced fatherly authority. But Adam didn't listen to him. And when Dan reached out to take Adam from Mirra's arms, Adam punched him in the nose. A little trickle of bright red blood debuted out of Dan's left nostril. He reached for his linen handkerchief, the one she had ironed and so carefully folded and placed in his breast pocket that morning, and used it to halt the flow.

"Goddamn it, Adam," Dan said.

"Don't you swear at him," said Mirra.

"Oh, hey Mirra!" called Charlotte's friend's mother from down the block.

Shit, thought Mirra. She turned to smile through her teeth.

"Everything all right there?" said the mother. She was dressed head to toe in Prada. She looked serene and calm, like she'd just had a massage.

"You know, terrible twos," said Mirra as Adam tried to stuff his fist down her throat.

"I thought you said he was three," said the mother.

There was a pregnant pause while Mirra glared at her, and then the woman said: "Well, we'll see you at the school auction," and gave a little ladylike wave goodbye as she headed downtown, hand already in her pocketbook to search for her cell phone, probably readying to call some other mother to gossip about Mirra's obvious misfortunes.

"The little bastard, he could have broken my nose," Dan said, gazing at his handkerchief like he'd never seen blood before. "Who was that woman?"

"Don't call him that. He's upset," said Mirra. Adam looks, she thought, just like how I feel. "She's one of Charlotte's friend's mothers."

"I know he's upset," said Dan. "But this behavior is unacceptable. Maybe we should just call and cancel."

"We can't cancel now," said Mirra. "We'll never get another interview. I can't believe you, Dan, I . . ."

Husband and wife stared angrily at each other. Drastic times call for drastic measures. Dan reached into Mirra's purse with disdain, as she held his eggbeater of a son away from him, and pulled out their secret weapon.

. . .

The interviewer was a woman named Mrs. Wallace. Her husband and her two boys had attended the school as children; she'd volunteered for years, she said, before getting a job in the admissions office. She wore flesh-colored stockings, Pappagallo flats, and something vaguely reminiscent of a St. John suit, tweedy and buttoned and boxy. Dr. Eichler and his wife, Mirra, sat on the brown leather couch, with their son, Adam, on his mother's lap. The walls were covered with pictures, and several of the bookshelves were lined with little porcelain figures, all in the shape of pigs. Mrs. Wallace collected pigs, she told them with a little laugh, sitting down in a damask-covered rocker. After the usual pleasantries, Mrs. Wallace leaned forward and tried to make nice with little Adam. "How old are you, Adam?"

No answer.

"So I hear you have two charming older sisters?"

Nary a sound. How could there be? Adam couldn't talk. And he had both a pacifier and a bottle in his mouth. His parents' secret weapons. It was the only way Mirra and Dan could think to calm him down. Adam was all plugged up.

"He doesn't usually take a bottle or a pacifier anymore. I, I, I guess he's just a little anxious," Mirra stammered.

"Of course," said Mrs. Wallace, "we are keenly aware of how trying new situations can be for little boys."

"Thank you for understanding," Dan said.

The adults smiled warmly at one another.

Mrs. Wallace leaned in close to Adam again.

"You know, Adam," said Mrs. Wallace, "if you come to this school, you're going to have to leave your pacifier and bottle at home."

Adam smiled at her, his adorable little smile, and the pacifier slipped out. Mirra's heart began beating rapidly. Mrs. Wallace smiled a Cheshire Cat grin. Emboldened, she reached for the bottle and gently twisted the nipple out of his mouth.

"Now, see what a big, handsome boy you could be?" said Mrs. Wallace.

Adam reached out and inserted the bottle back in his mouth. This time, Mrs. Wallace tugged more firmly. It came out with a little pop.

"Shut yer piehole," said Adam.

In the initial moment of shocked silence that followed, Mirra's heart swelled with pride. The woman was a cunt. Her little boy had put her in her place. He had shown strength, resolve, confidence, confidence, confidence. It was only when the reality of the full horror of the moment began to dawn on her that she recognized Adam for the traitor that he was.

He could talk.

. . .

The fat letter of acceptance arrived at the Eichlers' apartment in the spring. But Mirra no longer lived there to receive it.

THE
SHABBOS
GOY

We were in Paris all of three weeks, my baby girl and me, when we saw our first bride. Without my cat-eye glasses, from afar she appeared even farther away, the world's teeniest bride, like a miniature pony. Upon approach, however, it quickly became clear that she was merely a child, probably only around four or five years old, a wafting meringue with legs. The family that followed were obviously Orthodox Jews, the father's black suit a slim elegant contrast to her pearly float, his wide-brimmed fedora girded by a satin band, but even still, I thought: Is she taking communion? Because the little girls in my neighborhood back in Brooklyn often dressed this way, in tiers, when receiving their initial sacrament. Only when a pudgy older sister followed in an identical halo of tulle and the helium of her own high spirits did I realize that both girls were simply members of a wedding, and that I now lived down the street from a synagogue, from which the conventionally proportioned female newlywed was at that moment making her royal exit. The doors were guarded by two telltale gendarmes, in riot gear and sporting automatic weapons.

THE SHABBOS GOY   **131**

The next afternoon it rained, but when I took my daughter out grocery shopping—me in my plastic yellow boots, the human cupcake safe and dry in her Snugli—I spied through the silvery murk another sylph in white, exiting the sanctuary and entering a convertible parked outside the temple, glumly holding an umbrella over her veiled and golden head. Soon it was about a bride a day, a never-ending pageant of women eagerly entering the world of marriage, one I had painfully, but most willingly, left behind.

After the divorce, after I'd picked up the handsomest sperm donor I could find at a bar in Red Hook, after I'd struggled with nursing the baby while navigating the IRT from Brooklyn College (where I eventually got fired for sleeping with a student) up to Columbia (where the same transgression inspired no official response), after teaching eleven courses a year as an itinerant adjunct professor finally killed my love of literature and, well, my love of people in general, my old camp friend Maggie asked me to come help her liquidate her English-language bookstore. She had married a Parisian, a cute jazz musician she met on her junior year abroad, given birth to four kids, now almost fully grown, and lived her girlish dreams. Her children spoke English with mellifluous French accents, they dressed with flair and all drank wine responsibly, and over the years when I visited, I had often coveted Maggie's life, full of books and music, thin thighs and rich desserts, unpaid bills and her husband's girlfriends. When one of these *femmes* became pregnant with twins, that ended some of that. E-books undid the rest.

The bookstore, A Moveable Feast, was located in Le Marais, the third arrondissement, traditionally the Jewish quarter, now a mixture of the LGBTQ crowd, well-heeled artists, and a daily influx of shoppers, much like the Lower East Side of Manhattan or Prenzlauer Berg in Berlin—lots of trendy cafés, galleries, and stores, with a few remaining kosher bakeries, falafel, and Judaica shops for the rapidly dwindling holdouts. It was tucked away in a little medieval cobblestoned plaza (which hadn't been so great for sales, but was big on charm) and was as tiny and crammed and disordered as the last several years of Maggie's life—and mine—so while we cataloged and boxed the stock, we often brought the stack of hardcovers outside just to make sense of them. I kept a plastic Exersaucer on hand for my daughter to spin in; it was unisex green with little stuffed dolphins affixed to the sides like carousel horses so she wouldn't get any princessy-pink ideas; I'd scattered some fabric books to bite on along the plastic trough that encircled her, and a handful of French Cheerios (*au miel et aux noix*) for her to chase down. This way I kept her close by my side as I worked.

Since I'd last seen Maggie, she had grown very thin—with her red hair tied loosely back and her freckled, bony chest she looked like a Walker Evans, a result, I'm sure, of all those cigarettes and misery—so I often stopped at the boulangerie on my way over to the store in the morning and laid out an array of treats, *viennoiserie,* atop a mobile bookshelf to tempt her. It was only around 11:00 a.m. on this particular day, but it was unusually hot for May. Global warming. I'd rolled my sleeves and hiked up my skirt as I sorted and dusted. At some point I'd tied my curls into a seemingly hilarious topknot, using one of the baby's cleaner bibs—very *I Love Lucy.* Mag-

THE SHABBOS GOY   **133**

gie did a spit take whenever she came outside to cry or order me around, which I suppose made the outfit worth it. So I wasn't exactly in full flower when the rabbi actively did not approach me. Instead, he stood to the side and surreptitiously sorted through a pile of books. The venerating holy way in which he bellied up to our merch, like he was pilfering God's own private wet bar, proved that, whether it was cool for a rabbi to immerse himself in secular texts or not, he was indeed a reader, not a civilian.

"May I help you, monsieur?" I said. I supposed it would have been kinder to have let him do his thing alone in a lonely way, but I was bored. This was an English-language bookstore and that was pretty much all my French. *Monsieur.* Except for *Un autre verre de vin blanc, s'il vous plaît* or *Combien coûte cette putain de tomate?*

"No *merci,* madame," he said, with a slight bow. Caught off guard, and purposefully staring now at the fascinating cobblestones beneath us.

There was something familiar about him. It occurred to me that I had seen him before, so I asked: "Do you live on my street? Rue des Tournelles?"

I thought I spied a little light bulb turn on above his head right then, as if he were an old-fashioned cartoon character, with a flicker of an idea, or maybe I've gifted myself the observation in retrospect, hoping that I'd caused a filament to light. Whatever, he continued to glance downward, but he was somehow looking at me through his third eye. I could sense it.

"My shul," he said. "My street."

134 FOOLS FOR LOVE

"My street," I said. My game. My curiosity.

"Forty-two Rue des Tournelles," I said, and his neck, long and curved like an egret's, slightly stiffened.

"No," he said, incredulous.

"Yes," I said, impressed by his incredulity.

I noticed that the book he had been reading was poetry. Dickinson. *Pain has an element of blank.* It was a poem I'd tried to turn to while my marriage was disintegrating, but the words had shriveled and flown off the page like ashes. *It has no future but itself.* I shut the cover and returned it to the rack.

"Not that it matters, but are you Jewish?" The rabbi's English was thick with a Yiddishy French accent. A Semitic patois.

"No," I said. "I'm not."

I was used to this routine from the Jews for Jesus thugs who manned the entrance to my subway stop at home, but I didn't mind.

Because I was hot and lonesome and somehow perpetually furious, almost to entertain myself, I said: "Are you?"

He looked at me, startled.

"Not that it matters," I said.

I learned later, it was something he was trained *not* to do. Look me in the eyes that way.

His were an unearthly blue. An empyreal Caribbean hue, the shade of a sun-filled swimming pool in a magazine ad, made wavy by the perfumed page's highly reflective gloss. They did not belong to the topography of his face, nor to this dank and sweaty French courtyard, smelling faintly of piss and spilled wine and lined with mossy stones, mushroomy corners. In the distance I heard a splash, the entrance of a dive, the sound of my solitude being knifed aside. A cleansing spray of hope atomized up my spine. For a moment, I thought we were both going to laugh aloud. The moment passed.

"I am a superhero," the rabbi said, with a raised eyebrow. "Disguised as an Orthodox Jew."

He wiped at his forehead with a broad white hankie. He was young, I saw, beneath his beard. Quite a bit younger than I was. Maybe not yet thirty. He had those handsome blue eyes, but his skin was pasty under a lustrous sheen, like a piece of marzipan with a hard sugary glaze. He was wearing so many clothes and the sun was so hot that he looked as though he might pass out. The rabbi smiled weakly. "Menorah Man," he said, but he seemed to waver in the currents of heat that emanated from the pavement as he said it.

"Sit, Menorah Man," I said, gesturing toward a chair. "You look dizzy."

He protested as he sat. But sit he did.

"Eat," I said, and I pointed to all the goodies scary-skinny Maggie had turned down: *pain au chocolat pistache,* almond croissant, and those creamy, crunchy, swirly things—I forget now what they called them, something yummy *aux raisins*? Escargot!

He said, "No, thank you," but reached for the gooiest, most chocolaty treat of all, a brioche that oozed molten dark brown lava, some vanilla crème, and the faintest architectural remnants of melted chips. Before he bit in, he asked: "Is it kosher?"

"Sacha Finkelsztajn?" I asked, referencing the landmark Jewish bakery from which the baked goods were locally sourced. It seemed kosher.

"Sacha Finkelsztajn," he said, and, as if all his problems were solved, he took a deep, satisfying bite.

We couldn't help ourselves, the rabbi and I; we caught each other's gaze and cracked up. That eruption of belly laughter! My daughter's eyes widened, startled by the sound. Poor baby. It was new to her.

"So, Mr. Superhero. Any women on your squad?" I knew full well that I was flirting, but that is something that I do, naturally, without thinking. It's the way I am. Just not usually with rabbis. Not that I'd ever had the opportunity before.

"Dreidel Maidel," said the rabbi, chewing thoughtfully. The chocolate was clearly reviving. The color was returning to his cheeks, reflecting the red in his damp side curls.

"Are you serious?" I said.

"It's a serious business," he said. "Acts of human kindness. Making mitzvahs. Hard to manage without the help of a righteous woman."

A righteous woman. Who was that? A grown-up person of the female gender? One who was good, decent, merciful, virtuous, and kind?

"Ah," I said. "But you have seen right through me. She is my alter ego."

He looked skeptical for a moment. Which I suppose I deserved.

"Something has to be done about my karma," I said, more honestly than I'd meant to.

THE SHABBOS GOY   **137**

"Karma," said the rabbi. "Not an innately Jewish concept, but then again within Judaism there is room." Here he quoted by heart, "Hillel saw a skull floating on the water. He said, 'Because you drowned others, they drowned you; in the end, those who drowned you will themselves be drowned.'"

"I mean I need to perform acts of human kindness, like you said. It would be better for us." I pointed at my kid. The dusky rose of her cheeks. Big black eyes. Her inky curls. Caramel-colored skin so rich I was often tempted to sneak a lick off the brown sugar of her neck.

"Need?" he said, something in him brightening. "That implies that you would find it beneficial . . ."

Yes, I nodded. I was in it for the benefits.

"My congregation," said the rabbi. "We could use some assistance. This very weekend. In your very building. From a Gentile." Again, he shook his head at the coincidence.

"Not that it matters," he and I said, in unison.

The baby laughed. She clapped her hands. The rabbi and I laughed, too.

. . .

A few days later, the rabbi came again to the bookstore. Maggie and I had almost finished putting the last of the poetry paperbacks in boxes, and we had a little red wagon out front where we placed them. Thierry, her second eldest and my favorite of all her offspring, six feet tall now and ludicrously handsome, was to ferry this precious but humble cargo by hand across the bridge to the Île de la Cité and then over to the Left Bank. Poor kid, last November he had spent the night of his eighteenth birthday on a restaurant's tiled floor listening to terrorists with machine guns massacring patrons in the café next door. For weeks, Maggie wouldn't let him out of her sight, but now they were hovering around a new normal. Today, his destination was Shakespeare and Company, one of the last English-language bookshops in Paris to endure. It was a place where print lived, wild and free, as it once had done at A Moveable Feast, and writers and readers still roamed. The bookstore was run by a young couple, so lovely and kissed by God they didn't need to do one more thing to improve their karma, but that did not appear to stop them. They'd offered to purchase Maggie's remaining stock.

The rabbi was wiping his face with a hankie. "Is it that hot out?" I asked. This morning had felt cooler.

"Some hoodlums, they spit on me as I crossed Rue de Rivoli," he said, looking both embarrassed and upset.

"Who?" I said. "Oh my God," I said. I picked up my bottle of Evian. "Would you like to use this to wash up?"

"Paris is getting worse and worse for us. I've soaped my face three times already," he said. "But still, I feel it on my skin."

It wasn't like I was stupid; I knew things sucked for the Jews in France. I had eyes; I saw the swastikas painted on the Shoah Memorial when I took the baby to the Île Saint-Louis for ice cream. I'd seen that video, *10 Hours of Walking in Paris as a Jew,* which followed a middle-aged man, wearing jeans, a sweater, and a yarmulke, traversing multiple arrondissements in one day, while being cursed at, kicked, and shoved by random people he passed. But now it was my very own rabbi being hurt.

Nervously, he picked up a volume off the top of the pile—he could not control his hands—and in an effort to change the subject, I supposed, offered to buy it. "I have the original at home," he said, "I am curious about the translation." Anna Akhmatova's *Twenty Poems,* converted into English by the poet Jane Kenyon.

"When I used to read, she was one of my sad favorites," I said.

The rabbi stared at me with his kind blue eyes. "Used to?"

"It is too painful and annoying now," I said. "All that useless truth and beauty."

"Useless? For me, literature has the power to heal." He sighed here heavily, I supposed, at the burden of a statement somewhat blasphemous. "It was Kenyon who wrote about her dog: 'Sometimes the sound of his breathing saves my life.'"

"When I first read that poem, I ran out and adopted a puppy," I said. Like the husband, he didn't last long.

"What is the price?" the rabbi said, discomfited I'm sure by his confession and the weirdness of the moment, but I pooh-poohed him.

"Don't be silly," I said. "Please, I insist. Take it as our gift." And then as if I were a windup monkey and someone else were talking, "You'll have to let me know if Kenyon does justice to the Russian."

"I will," said the rabbi, looking again at his book, ah but for that third eye. "Now, about Friday night . . ."

He took a deep breath. This spiel of his would take stamina. "Elvis Presley," he said, which wasn't where I expected him to start. "Martin Scorsese. American Christians, who at

140 FOOLS FOR LOVE

one point in time generously executed the services you are about to perform. According to the rules of Jewish law, it is possible for a non-Jew to complete certain tasks, which Jews are forbidden from performing on the Sabbath, having to do with labor, using electricity, handling money. I am told when Al Gore and Joseph Lieberman were in the American Senate, Lieberman, who was shomer Shabbos, would sleep on his couch in his office before Saturday votes, and Gore would turn the lights off for him. Your general, your Colin Powell, in his youth, too, lent such a caring hand to a Jewish neighbor he ended up fluent in Yiddish. Even the president of the United States"—here the rabbi could not wring the pride out of his gentle voice—"President Obama, did such charitable acts as a young man, with loving-kindness in his heart.

"I could never have requested this of you outright—a Jew may only accept the work of a non-Jew if it is of his or her own free will and for his or her own gain. But you volunteered."

Yes, indeed. Out of regret, existential fear, or maybe just ennui, clearly, I was ready to volunteer for anything.

He reached into his pocket for his handkerchief once more and wiped away at that indelible hateful spittle.

That next week, he said, a man and a woman were to be married in the rabbi's shul, and the bride's American relatives had rented a flat in my very building through the same website that I had, Paris Ooh-La-La! (Please note: That exclamation mark is the company's, not mine. I reserve my exclamation marks for important things.) As with many apartments in Paris, the outer door to the building was unlocked only by pressing a series of numbers on a matrix that then buzzed one inside. The lock itself was electric,

THE SHABBOS GOY **141**

as were the light switches I turned on by my footfalls as I ascended each stairwell landing. I could safely usher the wedding guests into the interior lobby, Friday dusk through Saturday nightfall, "Until three stars are visible," the rabbi said. After that, my services no longer would be necessary.

. . .

Although they had arrived earlier in the week, I did not meet the Grynbaums until Friday night. The mother was a specialist in infectious diseases, the father a pediatric oncologist. They seemed less religious to me than the rabbi—the father was clean-shaven and wearing a hat. I could not tell if the mother wore a wig or not. The four teenage boys sprouted more hair on their necks than on their still-soft, steamed-bun-white cheeks. A younger girl called Molly, maybe ten or eleven, her hair tied back in a minky braid, looked an awful lot like a Degas ballerina.

At around 11:00 p.m. they hollered up to me from the street, as they could not use the phone or the outside intercom. I leaned out the window in my T-shirt and sweatpants and waved. They thanked me so profusely when I came down the steps, my baby wide awake and ready to rock, and fussed over her so satisfyingly, that I practically swooned from all the attention. For so long, only Maggie had admired her.

"What a cutie-beauty," the mama cooed.

They were New Yorkers, like me. All five children went to a Jewish school on the Upper East Side. They were *thrilled* to be in Paris.

"The food," said the mama, "the wine! We haven't been here since Greg finished with his residency." They had had

142 FOOLS FOR LOVE

Shabbos dinner at their relatives' that very night and stayed out late talking. "We picked this place because it was in walking distance from my cousin," she said. "We didn't even think about the door code," and then she stifled a pretty yawn.

My cue, so I pushed the wooden door aside. We entered the stairwell, ladies first. At the ground-floor landing when I took a first magic step, a dim little hall light switched on automatically illuminating just the next stretch of staircase, and instead of cursing the darkness, I was suddenly grateful for the shortsightedness. Who cared about the long term? I could see enough of where I was going, not really wanting to know more. As I climbed those steep stairs, I thought that perhaps the move to France however temporary had been a smart one. I was helping Maggie. I was assisting this nice family. I was doing good.

. . .

The following Thursday, the caretaker at the synagogue fell ill with appendicitis, and the rabbi stopped by the store. I was deep in the stacks in the basement, boxing up the anthologies.

The rabbi came down the steep steps carefully, to ask me how it all had gone.

"They were so lovely, those Grynbaums," I said. "I'd do it again in a heartbeat."

"It is warm down here, reminds me of the sanctuary, without the fans," said the rabbi. "Too bad the caretaker won't be there tomorrow night to turn them on."

"*Bébé* and I can do it," I said, transformed into a person with purpose.

"*Bébé*," he repeated, delighted I suppose by my growing French vocabulary.

At this my daughter lifted her arms to him, and the rabbi automatically boosted her out of the playpen that I'd fashioned from dictionaries and a beat-up wooden desk I'd laid down fortlike on its side. I guess he was an old pro at picking up babies; he already had three of his own at home. He pressed his lips to her forehead and I watched her relax in his arms, returning his kisses to his chin.

"It's been a long time since anyone but Maggie or I have held her," I said.

Sometimes it is necessary to reteach a thing its loveliness, he recited.

"Kinnell," I said. "'Saint Francis and the Sow.' Are you even allowed to like that poem? It's so Catholic."

The rabbi shrugged. "It speaks to me," he said.

The words suddenly came back and I recited too: *To put a hand on its brow of the flower and retell it in words and in touch, it is lovely.*

"We like the same things," he said, bewildered. And then with one arm around my daughter, he put his other hand shyly to my brow, I suppose to remind me that I too was lovely. At that moment of supreme pleasure and recognition, I found my way into his and *bébé*'s embrace, by wriggling myself inside, and then as preposterous and natural—both—into the path of each of their lips.

When eventually we shyly parted, he whispered heartrending words of apology. But I waved them off. No need. I was glad for it all, and not sorry one little bit.

. . .

After that, the rabbi came to me toward the end of the day several times a week, to instruct me on the congregation's needs during Shabbos. I might light the pilot light of an elderly couple's oven. I could be entrusted with a last-minute errand to pick up a forgetful bridesmaid's matching lipstick. If anyone needed groceries or medical supplies, I was their Dreidel Maidel, as I could handle money. When payment for my deeds was involved, it came to me in advance so that it felt like a gift instead of labor. But all of it felt to me like a gift, the payment, the work, the blessing of being able to help make a mitzvah for someone else, supporting the rabbi, being in his company.

There in my apartment, before evening services, the baby napping in the Pack 'n Play by my bed, the afternoon court-yard light streaming into the bedroom, he would read to me out loud from the Russian poets, Tsvetaeva, Mandelshtam, and Pushkin, in English and then in Russian, his grandmoth-er's native tongue. *When you're drunk it's so much fun— / Your stories don't make sense. / An early fall has strung / The elms with yellow flags.* Akhmatova wrote this for the Italian painter Modigliani, when they were lovers in Paris, their spouses out of sight and out of mind. Reading together this way was so intimate; I suppose in a sense we too were having an affair. I mean I had made a couple of passes at him, but it was a no go. "I am married." He'd whispered this in my hair. But it didn't really matter. Sex I could get anywhere. "I have a good wife," he'd said. "But we married so young . . ." And in the fading white jet-stream trail of his sentence, I imagined her as a baby bride herself, like the child I first saw on Rue des Tournelles, someone beyond envy.

. . .

Finally, when there was nothing at the store left to box, sell, or give away, Maggie and I decided to throw a goodbye party, inviting the workers, our customers, the expat writers who'd crammed the packed aisles during readings with their tiny audiences of friends and former students, and local alcoholics looking for free wine. I wore a long white lacy dress I'd found during the *soldes*. I put my daughter in a sky-blue tutu. Maggie rocked a short skirt and a plunging neckline and stilts for heels—her twenty-some years abroad had taught her well; she looked startlingly good for someone who felt so awful, and she wisely began drinking at eleven in the morning. Soon she was dancing on that downstairs desk in those pretty red-soled Louboutins she'd purchased at Bon Marché when she gave up on paying rent—we'd brought the desk and the rest of the furniture out into the yard. François, Maggie's ex, even wandered over in the afternoon and ended up playing the piano until 2:00 a.m.

The baby and I talked and sang and drank, and if I kissed a famously sexy British writer, with the initials JD, who was there to know or care? At around three in the morning, François wisely took it upon himself to walk Maggie home—she was trashed and crying, mascara spider webbing underneath

146 FOOLS FOR LOVE

and above her lashes. How purely his arm fit around her waist. For Maggie, there was no tomorrow; the store was gone, she and the youngest of the four kids were flying out the next day to spend the rest of the summer in the States at her family's home in Michigan. I'd been invited, but I'd declined. The good people at Shakespeare and Company had offered me a job as events coordinator, but I wasn't sure if there was enough for me in Paris to stay on without my best friend. I had one week left on my sublet, so the clock was ticking, but isn't it always, ticking ticking ticking until it stops? *Look, just as time isn't inside clocks / love isn't inside bodies.* I quoted Yehuda Amichai to myself as I watched Maggie and François stumble together down the cobblestones. I silently wished them both a night of good sex and no backsliding.

Most of the crowd was gone now, the wine bottles and plastic cups out in the garbage bins, the trays of food long devoured. Besides the piano, the desk—which Maggie's sons moved back inside—and some empty shelves, there wasn't much left to steal, but I locked up the store anyway. Both JD and Thierry, Maggie's boy, with cougar lust in his eyes, offered to walk the baby and me home, JD even drunkenly proposed to put us up for a time in London, or was it Capri? But Paris in the summer, even with all the tightened security, is an all-night party, and I was sober enough and thus sensible enough, for me at any rate, to send them both on their way, with kisses on both cheeks.

The baby was sound asleep in the Snugli as we turned onto Rue de Tournelles, which was gray and empty and puddled, Parisian streets were always puddled, rainwater, urine,

THE SHABBOS GOY **147**

wine. The entrance to the shul was locked and blind to the street. The gendarmes had either gone home for the night or were themselves out at the clubs. I had not spent much time thinking about them, the strain or tedium of their work, what they thought about the threat to the congregation, to themselves, to their way of life. If they cared or not, if they cared desperately. It was overdue, but I thought about them then.

Up ahead across the street was the heavy wooden door of my building. On the other side, my side, was a religious man I knew.

"It's so late," I said.

"I was worried about you getting home," the rabbi said. "But then I saw you brand-new in your white dress . . . Like one of our own brides." His voice flooded with relief, but it was also somber. "I've come to tell you that my family and I are leaving. My uncle found us a congregation near him in Miami Beach. There is no safety here for the children."

I nodded. Children come first.

"They threw garbage at Rachel on the street, with the baby in the carriage. My older boy was teased and tormented on the Métro. There was a bomb threat at the school. One of the teachers was stabbed as he was walking home."

His eyes were so sad. The world was a cracked plate. At any moment it might shatter completely.

The baby stirred against my chest. The rabbi put his open palm on her head, almost as if he were giving her a blessing. *"Hope" is the thing with feathers,* the rabbi said. Dickinson again. Then we kissed for the second and last time, and before I had a chance to beg or thank him or even punch him in the nose, he walked away in the direction of Place des Vosges, toward his home and his apartment, I assumed, but I didn't even know where that masked man lived.

The baby and I crossed over to our building.

I entered in the door code, but I must have forgotten the numerical sequence. So I tried again, and then again, scrambling the numbers up, for minutes it seemed, and while I fumbled I thought, Now that I am nobler, almost a righteous woman, what is next for us? The sky grayed and pinked, and in the clear light of day, it was my baby and me, alone again, but in Paris. Beautiful, anti-Semitic, terrorist-ridden, xenophobic Paris. On the other side of the river there was a bookstore and in that bookstore there were books and work, if I wanted them.

With a whoosh, the numbers came back to me: 54321.

Duh.

I plugged them in and the door opened.

I AM
SEVENTY-FIVE

Six months after her husband died, Lily Weilerstein found his sex diaries buried in the back shelf of the cedar closet in the hallway of the Upper West Side apartment where they had lived together for almost forty years, since the "Age of Possibility" as Walter referred to it, back when they were almost young.

Their first place had been a railroad flat, four flights up, three avenues over on Columbus, amid the drug dealers and the prostitutes, the opera singers and the social workers, fine for newlyweds starting out. But when ten years into the marriage Walter had found an ad for a sublet on Riverside Drive hanging on the bulletin board at the union where he worked, Lily had thanked God for it; or, better yet, God's secular equivalent (luck). She was eight months pregnant with their third child at the time. Three bedrooms and a maid's. Who was the maid? Lily? Walter?

In the beginning they each took turns scrubbing the floors and the toilets. Activists, every year they renegotiated their marital contract in the spirit in which they embraced their life's work—"To each according to his abilities, to each according to her needs." Walter needed more than Lily did, this much was obvious, and so that little cupboard of a maid's room quickly became his study—a room of *his* own—leaving Lily only a corner of the dinner table for her leaflets and her tower of files (political campaigns, abortion rights, the PTA, a *real* job as a family advocate in an assemblyman's office, then that dazzling move on up to Chuck Schumer's). But the cedar closet, that was Lily's turf; and for her it spelled out luxury.

Now, forty-some-odd years later, Lily was on tippy-toe on top of an ancient stepladder, breathing in the must of rotting papers and old photographs, the stale air of wool mufflers and winter coats, the rich red wood having long ago squandered and released its scent; she was searching the high shelves for one of Walter's gray cashmere V-neck sweaters, actually thinking the stupid soft thing might smell like him and give her comfort—what a moron! She had been grieving him at the time. But once Lily opened the first in a series of eight spiral notebooks—just the sight of Walter's handwriting had made her gasp, his elegant European penmanship exhibiting such a striking physical lyricism that Lily could almost hear the swelling musical accompaniment, those telltale strings— she realized the treasure trove she had uncovered.

Like a sleepwalker, she carried the notebooks into the bedroom. There she lay on their queen-size bed, paging through the riveting, devastating accounts of Walter's shenanigans—feet up, belly down, the same posture she'd adopted when she'd read movie magazines as a teenager in her father's house in East New York—hunting frantically for something to make her feel better.

Thank God, Lily thought, she had been included, referred to throughout as "my beloved, my one" in the entries. Walter's determination of their not-infrequent couplings had been quite accurate: "sweet, loving, a physical home." During the long, involved course of their marriage, she and Walter had had a real romance; they fought and laughed and talked incessantly, on the phone, at the kitchen table, in the bathroom while he shaved and she sat on the toilet to pee. She'd counted on the fact that they'd loved each other always. The damn notebooks had done nothing to dispel that notion. But clearly they had not had the hot, exciting, dangerous, truly erotic sex that Walter had so evidently been drawn to.

Names, dates, positions; her friends, his friends, her own first cousin, Ceil, long dead now, from cancer of the breast—beautiful, neurotic, unmarried Ceil had schtupped her Walter! And a smattering (this stung particularly, although she wasn't quite sure why) of citations of liaisons with men, some referred to by initials, some by number, men from bars, public lavatories, men from trains, business trips—Walter had been a labor lawyer, he was always off somewhere protesting something, saving the world, she'd thought, and sucking, it appeared now, some teamster's cock. As soon as she'd uncovered her husband's secret life, Lily didn't mourn him any longer.

Instead, once she'd laid her eyes on the messy by-product of a complex, human existence—Walter's—Lily was jealous and competitive and bent on getting even. If Lily had not had this amazing sex with Walter, she'd not had it with anyone.

Such words he used! For desire alone: *lustfulness, goatishness, horniness, libidinousness, lasciviousness, hot blood, hot pants,*

152 FOOLS FOR LOVE

and *hot rocks*! Why, his descriptions of the female organ were almost embarrassingly adolescent—*like a pink oyster, a wet flower, a warm glove.* But for the male jeweled set he chose the rough-and-tumble *bag and basket.* How he reveled in his clandestine role as archivist, as diarist, that adulterer.

They had been married for fifty lovely years. And three lousy ones. The lousy ones coming at the end, after Parkinson's had taken hold and Walter's hands had first begun to shake and then his balance had faltered and finally he was reduced to taking little mincing baby steps like that character Tim Conway used to play on *The Carol Burnett Show.* One night, when she was sound asleep—caring for him had exhausted her so!—Lily had woken up abruptly to the sound of a large thump, her Walter falling and hitting his head on their hardwood floor. He'd suffered a massive cerebral hemorrhage, and with their three grown children surrounding her—one flying in from LA, one from London, the other hopping in a cab across town—he'd undergone two bouts of neurosurgery the next morning. A month in the hospital and another three in rehab had brought him home, home to a life of wetting the bed, spilling food, and a lot of incomprehension; it had been incomprehensible to Lily that the man she had spoken with nonstop for half a century now had so little to say. It seemed incomprehensible to her that the golden old age they had planned for—Elderhostel, a trip to China, together always together, protesting whatever horrible mess came next—had been taken away from them. It had seemed incomprehensible to her as she bathed and dressed Walter and schlepped him from one form of therapy to another that this was the manner in which her brilliant, desirable, always-interesting, somewhat-difficult husband would end his life.

But of course that is the way it ended; after three miserable years, he'd had a series of seizures in their bed as she frantically called EMS, and then died, just died there in that same bed, a bed they had shared for so long, a bed where she had nursed him and slept with him and watched TV with him and read to him and fought with him and made up with him, *the bed she was lying on right now!* He died on their bed with a miserable, twisted angry expression on his face that actually held more intelligence than she had seen in it for a long, long time. In death, his face was accusatory. It said: *Why did you let this happen to me?*

It had been an expression she had tried to erase from her mind. At present, she nurtured its memory.

Lily rolled over, now, onto her back, away from her husband's meticulous ledgers, and tried to capture her breath, which along with her heart, these days, had the habit of running away from her. On the ceiling of their room, there was a rather large water mark and an accompanying crack and fissure. It was in the shape of the city of Tallahassee. Was this blemish somewhat new, or had it, like the rest of the decay in her life—the age spots that bloomed like lichen across the top of her hands, the foreshortening plait of her spine—been stealthily creeping up on her?

Lily made a mental note to look into the fissure's origins. Her second-generation upstairs neighbors—the building was rent controlled—a family of five, had long ago moved to the suburbs (Ridgefield? Scarsdale? Montclair!) and used

154 FOOLS FOR LOVE

the seven-room apartment as a pied-à-terre, so it was largely empty. She could try and summon the new super, Fred, whom she'd met only through an announcement slipped under her door. He didn't answer his pager and was therefore never around when she needed him. Household upkeep, and the wrangling of craftsmen, had been Walter's responsibility, one he'd acceded to Lily with regret when illness had left him no longer competent. Not that he was handy by nature; Walter wasn't, he was an intellectual, a campaigner, an advocate—his was a life of the mind! (And now, it seemed, of the gonads.) But he hadn't relished handing over any part of his domain, even the aspects that he most despised.

She was old. This fact was incontrovertible. Lily was old and would die soon. She sat up. All the blood rushed from her head. She placed her palms on the bedspread to steady herself. She looked at her left hand, with the simple silver wedding band—she and Walter, they'd had such ideas! they'd had such purpose!—and she watched as the swollen blue veins rolled over the thin piano wire that played her fingers as she stretched them out. She stood carefully, and then when she'd regained her balance, Lily walked out of her bedroom and down the hall, past that stupid cedar closet, kicking the door shut, and into the kitchen.

There she opened the refrigerator, poured herself some organic Georgia peach juice she kept around for the grandkids. She sat down at the kitchen table, knocking the fat brown calico cat, Buster, off his smug little square of sunshine. She moved her own head and shoulders into it, resting on her elbows. The light that emanated from the interior courtyard (the windows here blessedly south-facing) bathed her kitchen and bathroom and the two children's bedrooms, which long ago had been converted into a guest room and a TV room—Lily and Walter, a TV room, what a laugh; they never had time for TV, not unless you counted CNN and *60 Minutes,* although in the end, she'd found herself watching Oprah for company—she loved that southern light! The sunshine felt good on her face, and for a moment she rested.

Then she reached an arm back into the cabinet where she kept the booze, opened a little airplane bottle of vodka, and put it in her juice.

Her husband was dead. She couldn't tell on him to his mother and swing Mrs. Weilerstein around to her side, or confide in her own angry, ever-humiliated father, who might have gone after Walter with a kitchen knife, because Pop had gone after her sister Rina's first husband with a kitchen knife when Rina had found him with the cleaning lady. They were all dead: Mrs. Weilerstein, Lily's pop, Lily's sister, her sister's first husband, Myman, and her second husband, Paul, dead, dead, dead, and, thus, in a conspiracy against her. Lily was on her own.

She drank her peachy screwdriver in one long voracious gulp. She would live without them, all of them, the bastards.

Lily picked up the phone. She dialed the number of her eldest daughter, Mirra. The wanton, wild one. The slut.

"How do I live without them?" Lily asked.

Three times a week, on average, in the last six months, Lily had called her daughter with this question. She stared at the Nature Conservancy calendar that she'd taped up to the kitchen wall as she asked it. It was April. Flowers and showers. So what.

Mirra had been booted from her own home by her own husband a couple of years back, caught once again, this time on her third go-round, with a younger lover. (She had her father's genes! It was hereditary! If only Lily had known this, she wouldn't have bothered spending so many years blaming herself. Mirra's promiscuity was the provenance of her father. *She's your fucking fault, Walter!*) Mirra's three children had spent the last few years doing a shuttle-bus route between their parents' apartments, for the boy East Side to West, and the two girls, a car service up from the Village. Mirra had discovered, she'd say on good days—on the days when *she* wasn't calling Lily up and asking: "How do I live without them?"—that the only way to have a life *and* children was divorce. All the pleasures of motherhood and still every other week one could sleep in, read a book, have sex, go to the gym, eat out, see a movie, talk on the phone, maintain a career. Mirra had once been a divorce attorney but was now in-house counsel at a bank. (Fieldston. Buck's Rock Work Camp. Oberlin College. A volunteer in a food pantry in one of the poorest sections of Colorado. And now a banker! Where had they gone wrong?)

"What's 'live'?" said Mirra, slightly irritated, chewing gum. It was an every-other Sunday, so she was on duty, and Mirra was always testy when she was on duty; she loved being with her kids in the abstract. In the background, World War III raged on between Lily's grandchildren. On a day this gorgeous, they duked it out inside the apartment.

Lily would bet money the windows were all closed. "Be qualitative, Mom. What exactly do you mean?"

"I want to get laid," said Lily. The vodka had gone to her head.

Now, Mirra cracked her gum audibly.

"Go to Florida," said Mirra.

It was good advice, but required preparation.

"Too far," said Lily.

"That's where the boys are," Mirra said. "At your age." She shrieked over her shoulder: "Lizzie Borden Junior, put that knife away. Now." She returned her attention to her mother. "You can't go to a bar. You're too old. You should dig up someone you used to know—some widower of a friend you always thought was cute, or a guy from high school, or the settlement house. City College. Recycling usually works for me. You could google. I googled Billy Rappaport last week, you know, from camp? And it paid off. He's divorced and a real estate agent living in New Jersey. He took me to Le Bernardin and spent oodles of money, even before I let him go to second base in the back of the Uber."

Mercifully, the line went dead. Lily hoped that one of the grandkids had yanked it out of the wall so that she wouldn't have to talk to that idiot Mirra any longer. The younger grandchild, the evil one, Adam. He probably did it. Adam was Lily's favorite.

The 92nd Street Y. That's where the old folks go when they're lonely. When they don't go to Florida, Lily thought, and they're not yet too demented. She'd never had time for all the stuff she'd read about in the Y's catalog, but she'd

158 FOOLS FOR LOVE

always title-glanced the descriptions, oohing and ahhing over the lectures she would never attend, the art classes she could not make room for. Now Lily had space for a lot of things. Like reading the 92nd Street Y catalog cover to cover. There were poetry recitations: a waste of time. There were concerts, which she loved, especially the strings, and lectures. There were one-day Italian-language immersions—how clever, one-day immersions, for her set this was commitment enough. She picked up the phone and registered for the language lesson. Then she hit the minis again and got drunk enough to fall asleep before the six o'clock news, in the TV room—she was not interested in her queen-size bed, where in 1987 Walter had apparently practiced his own fingering on Mirra's homely, overweight piano teacher.

He was an equal opportunity adulterer, that Walter. For a moment Lily allowed herself to miss his soft and generous heart.

. . .

The morning of Lily's first and last Italian class, she had a wake-up call in the shower. She realized she could hold her candle *in the looks department*! She had been grooming her body painstakingly—not that she expected anything to happen right away, she *didn't* expect anything to happen right away, she knew that these things, romantic things, take time, but she wasn't looking for love, she was looking for *sex;* and so Lily prepared herself for the possibility. Because sex, apparently, sex according to Walter—that's how she now referred to the notebooks in her mind, *Sex According to Walter*—could happen without even a cursory introduction.

She shaved her legs carefully across the Stiltony varicosities that mapped her calves and around the triangle of her pubic hair, silver now and sparse, and under her arms for the first time in months. Since before Walter died. Since way before Walter died. It took a while to do this. Her legs were still slim, but they were wrinkled, the skin fanned softly around her inner thighs in little pleated folds. She soaped her body carefully, each breast slippery and heavy as one hand lifted so the other could take a good swipe beneath and around it. She washed and conditioned her hair. When the water was off, she applied lotion to the soft moving mass of her skin, so separate now from the body beneath it. She'd taken tweezers to the dark down near her belly button, around her nipples, and then finally, daring the full-length mirror, around her chin. God. Then she'd stared for a good long time. Her breasts sagged, but they were still full, her skin was loose, but she wasn't fat, and oddly enough her body looked younger than her face and hands. Far less crinkly. Surely she could find someone to have sex with her, someone old and desperate, nearly blind. Surely some old codger would be glad enough with the help of Vaseline to stick his penis in her tushy, one of the many sexual acts Walter had clearly relished—he'd waxed on about it so in his notebooks—and yet had not ever *even once* attempted with his wife. Lily turned around and spread her butt cheeks and examined her anus in the mirror, its pretty pink pursed lips. There was nothing wrong with her in this department.

She wrapped herself up in a towel. Applied makeup and deodorant, brushed her teeth and her drying hair. Then she padded down the hall to her bedroom, where she did her level best to dress attractively. She wore jeans, regular jeans, not the grandma kind but the Levi's she'd been sporting since she'd admired them on the bodies of all those younger women at all those antinuke marches: jeans, short boots, a soft pink sweater. She first swept up her silver hair into a French twist, but the class was in Italian immersion; she wanted to look Italian! (Perhaps it had been a mistake to shave her armpits?) So she undid her hair and let it hang loose in waves around her shoulders. Was that too beachy and wild? She fastened the sides back into a princess-pony with a clip.

She'd been an attractive girl, with a good body, strong, large breasts, not-so-large hips. Over the years she'd thickened and then she'd slimmed; after Walter died she'd stopped eating. If same-sex dalliances had worked for her husband . . . Maybe a woman would be more forgiving. *A pink oyster, a wet flower, a warm glove.*

That's when the ceiling literally fell in. Or at least a great big chunk of it, a piece in the shape of the entire state of Florida. It fell in a shower of paint and plaster, missing Lily by inches, covering her and her outfit with dust.

It took Lily a moment to recognize what had just happened. The ceiling was now on the floor, the world had turned itself upside down, her outfit and her day and her rug were seemingly ruined—and yet she herself was not hurt. She pinched the back of her own thin hand, the skin tented and stayed that way, elasticity a thing of the past. She was alive, the fractured state of Florida in pieces all around her. So much for discovering the joys of homoeroticism today.

She was alive and alone with a mess to clean up, story of her life.

It was then that God spoke, or what sounded like God the way she had been *trained* to think of *him,* a masculine voice from on high, a mature contralto, stentorian.

"L—y, are you all right?"

L—y. Lily wasn't sure if the voice was saying *Lady* or *Lily,* the personal salute being that much more appropriate for an all-knowing deity, the other more suitable to the "great truck driver in the sky," and this, too, she found stunning.

She gazed heavenward and saw a hole amid the mess in her ceiling. In the center of the hole was an eye. It peered down at her.

"Perhaps a waterbed was not the best idea," said the voice, deep and resonant, the inflection of a radio announcer, presumably attached to that eyeball—the iris bright blue, framed by black lashes, that much detail surprisingly clear. It was then that Lily noticed the steady drip drip drip of water raining down on her bed. It was thickening some of the plaster into glue. "I was unaware of the leak, but I shall have it patched up in no time."

The situation was hurting Lily's neck, so she stopped looking up. Instead, she exited her bedroom in search of a plastic sheet to cover her ruined coverlet and a change of clothes for herself—both located in the cedar closet. The mirror in the hallway startled her: Covered in plaster the way she was, she looked already dead, white as a ghost.

She had just stepped out of her outfit, so carefully selected and hopefully donned—could a dry cleaner save that soft,

162 FOOLS FOR LOVE

pink sweater?—and into a vintage Diane von Furstenberg knockoff Mirra had bought Lily as a bribe after she was kicked out of high school for giving blow jobs to the math team, when the doorbell rang.

Perhaps it was Fred, the new super, here to rescue her. Lily walked to the front door, tying the wraparound dress shut, trailing dust. Maybe he would be her guardian angel.

When she opened it, an elderly gentleman, wearing a tie-dyed T-shirt and jeans, stood unshaven in her doorway, his gray hair long and curling about his ears, blue eyes light as morning sky, framed by dark, long, interferon-produced lashes, Barbie lashes, wasted on a fellow. It didn't take a rocket scientist to realize that this old guy was the owner of the waterbed upstairs. He was carrying a vacuum, a mop, and a garbage bag.

"Please," he said. "It's my fault, I didn't realize the valve was leaking, allow me to man the cleanup."

"Man" the cleanup? He could take over for all Lily cared, except who was he? She hadn't seen him before.

"Who are you?" said Lily.

"Forgive me," said the elderly gentleman. "Irv, Irv Gorenstein, I am Nathaniel Swan's uncle. They have been letting me stay in their apartment."

Nathaniel Swan was Lily's upstairs neighbor.

"Well, Irv," said Lily. "You've pretty much destroyed my bedroom. Now that there is a hole in the ceiling, I think we should call in the professionals, don't you?"

"Professionals, shmessionals," said Irv. "I've never been afraid of honest labor. I left grad school for the factories and the factories to work the rails! I've built bridges and I've built tunnels. I was a garbageman, a waiter, I registered voters. For one blissful summer I harvested grapes in France. I tended sheep on a commune in California, all this before I got my CPA." He was inside the foyer of her apartment. He was leading the charge to clean up. Before she could say a word, Irv Gorenstein was halfway down her hallway.

"Well, if you insist," said Lily, as if she'd had a choice. "But what about the flood upstairs?"

"Taken care of," said Irv, over his shoulder. "I lived in Florida for a long time, I did a lot of pool maintenance."

He was in her bedroom. She had no choice but to follow him.

"I was always stopping up leaks and mopping up deluges," said Irv. He said it to the ether; he didn't bother to look Lily's way. He was too busy righting wrongs, making reparations. He had a lot to make up for. "Too bad the hurricanes didn't wash that whole festering sore of a state away." He was grateful now for a task at hand, this much was obvious.

"Parkland! The Pulse nightclub! A twelve-year-old Black kid with a life sentence! People of color turned away from the polls! And all of them registered Democrats! Is this America?"

Irv was a gray-haired whirling dervish, an aged Deadhead spinning across her hardwood floor. (Lily knew from Deadheads, her middle child, Eric, had spent two years of his life on a drug-addled "tour." She and Walter had found him tripping his brains out in a parking lot in Red Rocks, Colorado, surrounded by hundreds of pathetic, lost children just like him. Hazelden. Recovery. Now he had his own freight-shipping company in Los Angeles. He was married with a mortgage and two kids of his own. Lily would never forget that evening in Colorado—Eric's pupils like concentric circles, his face as crimson as the enormous ridge of rocks that surrounded them in the glow of sunset—Walter picking the boy up like a baby, hoisting him over his shoulder, turning to her: "Lil," he said, "did you ever see such a color?" Indeed, the mountains looked like a slab of rare steak. A sensualist, even while rescuing his son, Walter had been overwhelmed by the gorgeousness displayed before him and was momentarily stopped by it. At the time, Lily wasn't sure if this quality made her love her husband more or gave her cause to hate him.)

Now Walter was dead, and here in her apartment was Irv Gorenstein, the aged hippie who'd probably sold her Eric his first tab of windowpane. Irv was lifting huge, soggy chunks of plaster and cramming them into the garbage bag.

"The duvet I'll send out to the dry cleaner's," he said. "They know me there."

"Okay," said Lily, but she was thinking: They know him there? Why? Because he does the deliveries?

"You should take a shower, shake the dust out of your hair," Irv said. "It's dimming the silver, obscuring the shine."

He'd noticed the shine in her hair! Lily's hand went to pat her head. Her palm met grit.

"Okay," she said, obediently, like a little girl, a little girl flattered and scolded, perhaps flirted with? She headed back into the bathroom, which was still damp from her shower of an hour ago.

Once again, Lily stepped into the tub. Once again, she let the hot water pound down upon her. In the rising steam, watching the swirl of dust collect around her drain, funneling downward like sand in an hourglass, Lily stopped to think: There was a man in her house, a stranger! She was naked and alone in the shower. Before fear or common sense kicked in, opportunity knocked. Perhaps this Irv would be her salvation. No guts, no glory, better late than never, blah blah blah and blah. To hell with Italian immersion. She'd save the fare on the bus crawling across the park.

Irv was in possession of a penis and his eyes were pretty. Lily stepped out of the shower and wrapped a velvety pink towel around herself, exposing her shoulders, the immutable beauty of her collarbone, her soft white arms.

She walked back into her bedroom.

Irv Gorenstein was still there, in Lily's boudoir, his back to her, his tie-dye like a bull's-eye around his potbelly, but from the rear, except for what appeared to be a little rattail of a ponytail, she could almost admire the strength of his slightly curving spine.

"Do you believe in love?" asked Lily.

Irv turned around slowly. "I used to," he said. "Back in my days at the commune." He paused and said sadly: "But three wives later and all that alimony, I learned that nothing comes for free."

"What'll it cost me, then?" asked Lily, aiming for insouciance, but hearing the little tremolo of desperation herself, as the words vibrated and caught on their journey out her throat.

"Are you serious?" said Irv. He was facing her now, black

166 FOOLS FOR LOVE

Hefty garbage sack in one hand, the hose of his vacuum in the other. He held it upright from the hip like a massive, silver hard-on. That bull's-eye belly! She'd have to do her best to put it out of her mind.

"Well," said Lily. "My husband is dead."

"I wish my wives were." Irv sighed. "Two of them joined forces and are sharing a condo in Palm Beach. For all their connubial pretense," he said, "I can't imagine that they're"—he put the hose between his legs and lifted one hand into the air to make bunny ear quotation marks—"'doing it.'" He sighed again. "Just a business deal to shake me down."

The misogyny! Lily thought.

"The other wife, my Jenny, she was my high school sweetheart and it was the miracle of my life that she came back to me! We re-met around the pool at assisted living. She was visiting her sister, Linda. We were only married for a few years, too young, too young, and so when fate once again brought us together, we decided we'd given up too early. But after the trouble, oy, all that trouble!"—here Irv Gorenstein sighed a guttural old Jewish man sigh, one time-traveling through him from another generation, a sigh that could not be ignored, it reminded Lily of her father's—"Even fat, sweet, loyal Jenny could not rise me from my torpor." He shook his head.

"Your bedroom," he said, "Look at that. It's almost spick-and-span. You need a new ceiling of course, and a professional carpet cleaner. I will personally buy you fresh bedding, a quilt, if you like, or I could make you one myself." He lowered his gaze to the rug.

"You quilt?" said Lily. If she were a man, she would have felt her own erection begin to wilt. "You're a quilter?"

"Life is all about reinvention," said Irv. "The question is how am I going to do it this one last time." He sat himself down on the corner of the mattress.

Oh God, no, thought Lily, is this the part where you whine on and on about your life?

"I need to get dressed now," said Lily. "You need to go back upstairs to your apartment."

"I didn't take my Viagra this morning," said Irv. "But I'm game if you are." He spoke to the floorboards. "You are a Democrat, right?"

"I'm practically a socialist," said Lily.

"I and others like me are the reason we are in this mess," said Irv. He put his head in his hands and began to cry. "I'm clinically depressed," said Irv. "As if you haven't noticed. The Viagra interferes with the Wellbutrin."

"None of this sounds very promising," Lily said. She was sure she'd never been so rude.

"Of course you disdain me," said Irv, between sobs. "I disdain myself."

"Oh, Irv," said Lily. Her whole life she'd been consoling men. The response was Pavlovian, the practice ingrained in her by her own mother, who spent much of her time pacifying her insecure and whiny husband.

"Now you 'Oh, Irv,'" said Irv. "But when you find out the truth, you will no longer bother to 'Oh, Irv,' me."

"What? What?" said Lily. "Don't make me guess. I'm too old, there's so little time. Where's the deal-breaker in this equation?" asked Lily. She was quoting Mirra, Mirra-the-banker on the phone.

"I'm from Palm Beach," he said.

168 FOOLS FOR LOVE

"So," said Lily.

He looked up at her. "So, the butterfly ballots? The morons who voted for Pat Buchanan? One of them was me."

Lily stared at him. "That was years ago!" she said.

"No, no, no," he said. "*I* changed the course of history! I'm one of the idiots who put Bush in the White House. And then what? 9/11. Iraq. Syria. The destabilization of the Middle East. All that death and destruction! Mass migration. The rise of nationalism. Without Bush, there would be no Trump. Without Irv Gorenstein, there would be no Bush."

"What about Obama?" said Lily.

"Obama," Irv said. "For eight straight years I was stoned on Obama."

He sighed again. That sickening sigh.

"At the end of the day, lovely Lily, it all begins with me," Irv said.

Lily considered this. There was both wisdom and insanity to his narcissism. Maybe it was valid, at this point, with all the ethical backsliding and hate-mongering, the about-face to bigotry and worship of money, to say that the life's work of the Irvs, the Lilys, and the Walters had been a waste of time. Her boy Eric had babbled on and on about the sand mandala when he was young and seeking. Tibetan Buddhists on their knees for weeks, crafting intricate floor paintings out of crushed gemstones, only to sweep them away after their glorious completion. Eric-the-junkie had intoned to his even-then-passé parents, old-schoolers bent on building systems that would stick, that the monks were celebrating the ephemeral beauty of physical existence. While he louchely lectured them from their worn-out sofa, the kid's chocolate-brown irises spiraled like brownie mix in an electric stand mixer. Be here now, said her poetic boy, her favorite, high that time on heroin.

No wonder Walter fucked anything that moved.

"I think you'd better go home," Lily said, readjusting her bath towel more snugly around her breasts.

Irv rose sadly to his feet.

"You shouldn't blame yourself," said Lily. "You'll feel better when you wash your face."

"Maybe," said Irv, doubtfully.

Lily handed him his vacuum and mop, picked up the garbage bag herself, and started their progress down the hall by giving Irv a little shove. She guided him all the way to the front door.

When she opened it, an attractive and fit man in black jeans and a black T-shirt, holding a tool kit, was standing on her doormat.

"Ahhh, Fred," said Irv. "You received my messages."

Fred's face did not move a muscle. It was carved, Lily supposed, out of a tea-stained wood. He looked like the statue of an angel from another civilization, perhaps one blessedly from the future? His green eyes glimmered for a moment, like there was energy pulsing deep inside him, although maybe it was the rich, red sheen of his glossy hair—the color of the interior of her cedar closet—that caused those eyes to glow. Or could be, they just flickered in amusement at the sight of this ridiculous geriatric situation? The one Lily regrettably and mysteriously found herself a part of.

"The problem is in the bedroom," said Irv.

Fred, lithe as a jungle cat, sidled past Irv in his tie-dye and Lily in her towel, and made his way down the hall.

"It was a pleasure to talk to you," said Irv, focusing now entirely on Lily. "You are a good person."

Good, shmood, thought Lily. Good never got anybody anywhere; but she said: "Thank you."

"Perhaps I can take you out sometime for a cup of coffee?"

"We'll see, Irv," said Lily. "God knows what's next for any of us. At this age I don't bother buying green bananas."

He brightened a little at the statement. He took the garbage bag from Lily's hand. Then Irv turned, also with his vacuum and mop, entered the vestibule and buzzed the elevator button.

Back in her apartment, in the bedroom, the mysterious feline Fred was eyeballing the hole in the ceiling.

"Some plaster should take care of that, no?" said Lily.

Fred turned his gaze from skyward to sideways, taking Lily in with those emerald eyes.

They stood this way for several moments, before Lily realized that her towel had slipped, exposing the left side of her chest.

Fred was staring at her breast.

Well, why the hell not, thought Lily. You only live once.

She let the towel fall to her feet.

(She'd seen this move many times in the movies!)

Later, when they were naked on the bed in the TV room, Fred having entered her from behind, one hand stroking her clitoris, the other cupped around her breast (Lily had half expected his body to be hairless, his crotch as smooth and seamless as a Ken doll's, but no, Fred was all man, all man in every department. She would tell this afterward to a proud, but envious "way-to-go Mom!" Mirra), Lily had felt the urge to cry out: *Oh Walter! How could you have forsaken me?*

But he was dead and Lily wasn't.

And so, her cri de coeur came out as one great, big, fat, satisfying moan of ecstasy.

IN A
BETTER
PLACE

We were driving back from a weekend away at a friend's house in Normandy when I thought I saw my father—his pebbly gray ashes indisputably scattered and sunk in the icy Atlantic ten long winters before—now alive and well, a passenger in a neighboring coupe. "Dad," I whispered in astonishment, like a little extra exhalation of breath. It was a word I hadn't uttered with ownership in years; it felt both primal and alien in my mouth.

My husband, at the wheel, swerved upon command when I called out, "Follow that car," as if he, Walker, were a taxi driver and we had just left one world and permeated a thin membrane of light and dark filmstrip into another: an old screwball comedy. Which in retrospect was what I suppose we had actually done, weaving in and out of traffic like that, giddily chasing the dead.

We'd recently moved to Paris, ostensibly for work. We rented our old pal François's place in Le Marais. François was a jazz musician Walker had worked with before, and he was in the US accompanying one of his late-life twins to wilder-

IN A BETTER PLACE **173**

ness therapy camp in Montana. Walker had a commission. He'd been asked by the Paris Opera to stage some performance art thing; he called it "a dance with voice." (Theater people love to speak simply; it's an inverse pretension.) My aged mother—poor thing—had finally died, by her own hand, to make the story sadder. She'd refused food and water, and although it may seem strange, what with all she'd lost (her marbles, her decorum), she maintained her divaesque ways. It took eleven operatic days of her screaming at yours truly to "kill me, already," which I could not bring myself to do, before her voice faded into a mumble, her arms reaching up to whoever was waiting for her on the other side.

(Unfortunately, a name and face don't readily spring to mind.)

Murdering one's own mother is simply against all the laws, *my laws, your laws,* I'm sure, including the ones pertaining to love, but that is not how she saw things. For the entirety of our lives, we'd lived on different planets. Even with the relief that partnered her last tortured gasp—those purple lips, the yellowing oily rind of her skin, the browned Natural History Museum set of teeth—*even at my age,* the loss of her untethered me from the earth. I was now the world's oldest orphan.

Still, as Walker gently reminded me, we were finally made free.

So with our beloved daughter Kate's support and encouragement, we sublet our apartment in the West Village to a lawyer friend of hers, and in the bubbling murk of Walker's and my collective unspoken truths (aka marriage) we flew, *flew,* from continent to continent across the black void of night, with the concrete surface of the ocean a mere death spiral below. The idea was not only to grab opportunity by its willowy throat but to see if Paris, that chilly, damp, lonely city, couldn't elevate my mood.

That is how we found ourselves on the road, stalking a ghost, on a carbo high from a bag of croissants, Walker momentarily morphing into one of those nutty European drivers—as he cut people off, he strangely seemed to be smoking and cursing in a Marseillais dialect—when we passed a tractor-trailer on the left and I got a better look in that red Audi. It was my father, all right. I knew his nose, prominent and hooked. When the life drained out of him, I'd watched it turn blue. Empty as a shell, his cadaver. I finally saw where he'd gone.

"Stay on his ass, Walker," I said.

Remarkably, he obeyed me.

. . .

This little side trip to Normandy had come after several months in Europe. An old producer of mine, from the LA days when I dabbled in screenplays, Felipe Elbazz, a chatty guy, a good egg, a rich good egg, had heard through the grapevine that we were in France and called to ask if we'd like to spend a weekend at his home in Normandy. They'd have to sell it off soon, Felipe said, he and his third wife, Yang, too expensive and self-indulgent a party prop in these hard times to maintain, but it was sitting empty and he thought it might be just the thing . . . Felipe uttered this last clause with an ellipsis. He had a heart, and a soft spot for the thing I do: spinning my life round and round in a blender and seeing what's left of it mounted on a stage.

So on a Friday afternoon, Walker and I rented a car and drove from the city, stopping in Giverny to give Monet's gardens a postcollegiate whirl and arriving later at the château than we planned. That huge old drafty castle was so crazy beautiful it could have cured anyone of anything. Except, apparently, me. There was a maid to greet us and serve us supper and a cook to cook, which she did—the meat, at least—over an open flame in the large hearth in the dining room. Saturday night, though, we were on our own, and since we'd gone to Bayeux in the morning to see the tapestry and to Mont-Saint-Michel to watch the tide recede and the mud bubble up, we were content to eat at a simple farm restaurant on the way home; that was lovely, too, the stone archways and wooden floors, the chicken and the duck, the Calvados and *tarte aux pommes.* Had Kate and her wife been with us—there was a delicate *omelette végétarienne* on the plat du jour—the dinner would have been perfect. We even had good sex that night, then slept apart in the twin beds, under heavy, dark oil paintings and acres of blue toile that drew residual patterns on the inner lids of my closed eyes.

But when I woke the next day, I didn't quite know where I was, still confused and misplaced in the world, perhaps, though filled with guilt-ridden gratitude for all the gifts that surrounded us, which for the life of me I just couldn't seem to enjoy.

In the morning, we sipped our coffee at the town bar, standing next to some still-drunk old men with their break-

176 FOOLS FOR LOVE

fast tumblers of red wine. Then we shopped at the tiny boulangerie next door, buying that aforementioned bag of croissants, the kind that shatter properly when torn, the butter rendering the folded puff pastry into thin yeasty layers of air and glass and grease, and hopped back into our car. We were on our way to see the beaches seventy years after they were covered in blood and boys, and long restored to their natural glory, when that little red Audi slid into the other lane. We tailed it in hot pursuit for a few minutes, but the traffic was so intense and full of like-hued cars we lost him almost as soon as I'd found him. My daddy.

"Who was it?" asked Walker, finally coming up for air— he'd been concentrating on the road that hard. "Can you see them up ahead?"

He was trying to make me happy. His curse. He'd wasted decades of his life this way. Probably he thought I'd spied a friend, or an unhinged Trumpist, or a famous actor we'd both worked with and still dined out on at industry dinner parties. How could I explain whom I'd actually seen without sounding totally insane? My father had taken a fall one night when he'd gotten up to go to the bathroom. Mr. Cardiac Infarction. All that aspirin. Two cerebral hemorrhages, two surgeries. He'd died in my arms, a long process of agonizingly paced stolen breaths, the fluid in his lungs, the ICU nurse suggested, drowning him.

"I thought I saw Brad Pitt," I said. "Sorry, Walky, a wild-goose chase."

Still handsome and brilliant, tired of me, beaten-down, teal-eyed, silver-haired Walker. He looked at yours truly now with disgust, anguish, pity—and a hint of boredom thrown in. He'd been here before.

"I'll treat you to a *grand plateau de fruits de mer*," I said, wanting to make it up to him. A tower of icy seafood.

"Anna," he said. All the sentences in his head came out encapsulated in that one word.

It's my name, Anna. Anna Herrera. I picked up the ethnic surname in a short heartbreak of a marriage, a name that has stood me well all these years, grant- and prizewinning-wise. Miguel, too, has been dead so long now it is sometimes hard to conjure up my first husband's striking face. We had tried to stay together, even though he couldn't stop sleeping with men, because we loved each other so very much. Such young, innocent knuckleheads. What an idiot I was.

Sometimes, Miguel and I would smoke dope and try sex with me on my stomach, my breasts hidden, flattened out, which helped sort of, but not much. That left breast that I worked so hard to hang on to a couple of years ago, I tucked inward, toward my heart, but it didn't prevent it from breaking.

. . .

Later that day, Walker ended up parking in a little public lot in Arromanches, a tiny port town just a few miles down the coast from Omaha Beach. We strolled past several war souvenir shops, on our way to the waterfront restaurant Felipe had recommended, stopping in one to peruse the offerings.

"Check this out," said Walker. "They have Prince Albert in a can." And so they did. Pipe tobacco that gave fodder to

178 FOOLS FOR LOVE

practical jokes from our parents' youth. "Got Prince Albert in a can?" "Then let him out." Ha, ha. Walker was amused. They had K rations from the war, still packed. "Enough botulism in one of these to freeze the foreheads of all of CAA," Walker said, somewhat bitterly. (Fun fact: Directors abhor Botox. One of the things Walker actually still likes about me is that I have a face that moves.) A pile of helmets and boots. On the wall above the cash register hung a photo of a GI, a Lucky Strike dangling from his smiling lips, being kissed on each cheek sandwich-style by two grateful old Frenchwomen, one with skin like mine.

"Do you think Kate and Lulu would like that as a souvenir?" I pointed to the picture. Kate's wife, Lucinda, is an activist who looks and dresses like a boy—she even has a little fuzzy blond beard that I have grown quite fond of. Kate also has a job she enjoys, working in internet PR, or we would have forced her and Lucinda to come visit already. It was hard to be away from our daughter for long. Kate's field is crisis management; I suppose that growing up with us, she'd come by her talents honestly.

Walker shrugged. "I think we can do better at the flea markets. I saw some opaline glassware there last week that kind of screamed the girls to me. Remember their last dinner party?"

How could I forget it? It had been so elegant. Lucinda cooked a daube for the meat eaters; Kate made some phyllocheesy thing. They'd seemed so happy, they inspired me. (It was after that night, in fact, that I booked our flight to France.) And so grown up! Kate sporting the diamond-stud earrings Lucinda had bought for her on their second anniversary. Black nails, red lips. Kate looking like a piece of candy.

"I'm famished," he said. "Aren't we in the land of Camembert aged in Calvados?"

We exited without a purchase and walked down a long alley, past several *moules-frites* shops, to the water. The restaurant Felipe had suggested sat on a boardwalk, directly on top of the sand.

The beach was flat and the color of a Siamese cat, camel and black and brown—the water flat, too, a dull pewter. Once upon a time, at low tide, the habit of the surf had been interrupted by brave young men flinging their bodies in front of bullets, willing to save the world.

At the outdoor terrace, Walker asked for a *table à deux*—a native Brit he speaks French, I speak "menu"—and the maître d' led us to a little round one, café-style, situated parallel to the sea. As he pulled out my chair and I took a seat, I noticed that across and to the left sat a good-looking woman at a neighboring table. She was in her forties, younger than me, African, wearing a long strapless sundress, her bare shoulders round and gleaming. There was a large green leafy pattern with bright orange flowers on the fabric, blossoms open. She shared a tower of fresh seafood on ice with her male companion, that same platter I'd promised Walker. Oysters on the half shell, boiled crab, large langoustines, tiny little cockles swimming in brine. She held an oyster out for her date to sup, and he leaned in, swallowing it whole, then pinkening like lobster meat over heat, smitten.

That nose, those skinny hands, piano fingers. It was my

180 FOOLS FOR LOVE

father. He'd been a surgeon before Parkinson's took that away, too. Now he wore a gaily patterned Hawaiian shirt. And the world's largest, goofiest grin.

"Dad?" I said. So, I hadn't been hallucinating on the highway, though I still couldn't believe my eyes. He was an old guy, yes, with liver spots, but not as old as he'd been when I last saw him. It was as if he'd been frozen somewhere around retirement. There was still hair on his balding head, and some of it was black.

"Sweet-chick," he said, a little sheepishly. "You found me."

I turned to Walker. Was this an acid flashback? Had I gone out of my mind? But he just shrugged. He'd seen it all, Walker's shrug said. We've lived together a long time.

"Hello, Howie," Walker said to my father.

"Walker, son. The two of you must join us," said my father. "It's a lovely feast."

That "you" and "us" nearly killed me.

"It's *treyf,* Daddy," I said. Unkosher. I said it lightly, without, I hoped, the meanness I felt in my heart.

"Shhh, honey," my father said, with a wink and a smile, looking up at the sky. "He'll hear you."

His lady friend laughed. She threw back her head, displaying her pretty throat. Clearly, she would hoot at anything, just to show it off. A swan's neck.

"This is Evangeline," said my father, introducing us. "We're in love," he said, as if that much weren't self-evident. "Being with her here"—his hand fanned out to encompass the sea, the sky, the wine, the food—"it's not hard. Before it was quite difficult, even with you, sweetie," he said to me. "My second favorite."

"You must be Anna," Evangeline said.

My father liked my older brother best. The gambler, my younger brother, not so much.

"She was a sweet girl," said my father, as if I weren't there. "But that crazy career. The *fagelah* she married. This one," he pointed to Walker. "Smart, but he could never make a penny. I had to pay for their daughter's school."

That last swipe at Walker burned me up.

"What on earth are you doing here?" I said. "Slurping oysters? All these years I've longed for you."

My father smiled. "Always a flair for the dramatic. That's your gift, honey. And you," he said, pushing it further with Walker, "how's the directing business?"

In his seat, Walker straightened his back, rising to his full height, which is tall, even in a chair. "Just fine. It's going swimmingly." He looked my father in the eyes. "That's a nice bottle of wine there, Howie," said Walker. It was a Muscadet sur Lie.

"What's mine is yours, Walker," said my father. "You know that."

Walker picked up the bottle and gave us both a healthy pour. He took a deep, indulgent sip. "I guess that's true," said Walker, slowly, the wine revving him up. "Your wifc was yours, then ours."

After my father died, we'd looked after her. For a while, when Kate was off at school, Mom had stayed in the tiny maid's room that had served as Kate's bedroom, until, even with help, we couldn't handle her at home. Things had gotten so bad sometimes she no longer knew who I was; worse, sometimes she remembered. The bedpans and the bedsores.

The diapers. Once in a while when I was feeding her, a rotted tooth would fall out of her open mouth.

Walker reached his hand out across the table and rested it on my right forearm, which like the rest of me was shaking. "That malpractice suit, the, ahem, 'screw-up' with your taxes, your drunkard son, and the other one, the greedy, bankrupt one. We seemed to inherit him, too."

He gestured toward my chest.

"We could have used your surgical know-how a few years back, me and Annie."

My father sadly shook his head.

"Walker, Walker, you know most lives end mid-sentence," Dad said. "It was that way with my parents, too. Muddles to clean up, scores and estates to settle. There's always more work to do."

"You don't look as if you're working, Howie," said Walker.

My father shook his head. He smiled ruefully, as if Walker were a child, which even now, in comparison with my father, he was. No matter how old we got, we would always be his children.

My father picked up the bottle. He poured us each another glass. We'd both inhaled the last round.

He turned to me, "What happened to your mother?"

"What do you think, Daddy?" I said. "She was beside herself without you."

"She played around with the will," he said. "That much I heard."

"It was a nightmare for Anna," said Walker, his face turning an inebriated red.

IN A BETTER PLACE **183**

"The boys are suing each other over your money," I said. "It's one of the reasons we fled to France. No forwarding address."

"Me too," said Dad. He and his Evangeline shared a private look and then they laughed and laughed.

"Your wife was the most destructive person I've ever known," Walker sputtered. "She took pleasure in our failures and was wounded by our success. She was conveniently noncompliant with her meds. Whenever Anna was opening a show, she'd go off them so we would have to rush back home to hospitalize her. Even Kate disliked her in the end . . ."

"Little Katie," my father said wistfully. "It would have been fun to watch that one grow up. Pretty and remarkably levelheaded. But maybe a bit too sensitive?" He shrugged a visible question mark.

"Yes, too sensitive." Walker nodded dryly. "She couldn't bear to watch *The Sopranos* because Tony's mother, who ordered a hit on her own son, reminded her of her own nan."

I handed Walker a glass of water and a cloth napkin. He took a sip, and then toweled off his face and his neck.

"Walky," I gently shushed him. This was my father, my battle. Already, I felt guilty enough for how much of my husband's rapidly foreshortening life had been sucked up by my family of origin's lunacy.

"None of us even speak," I said.

My father shook his head, sadly.

"How could you leave all that to me?"

My father reached across the table, taking Evangeline's hand in his.

"I'm in a better place," Dad said.

184 FOOLS FOR LOVE

. . .

When lunch was over, we bade our farewells. My father kissed me on my forehead, and he held my wrist, too, for a moment, until I realized he was taking my pulse, like he sometimes used to do when we all lived together back in Stuyvesant Town, so I shook it free. I was angry, sure, but that wasn't the half of it.

"I miss you, Daddy," I said, and meant it. I missed him more than I knew. I missed him so much I could feel the liquid in the center of my bones. More, I missed who I used to be back when I was still his daughter, a person with someone between her and God, a layer of protection floating like a cloud above me.

"It is what it is," said my father, the cliché king. "What can you do? Try to think about something good." Then he and Evangeline walked hand in hand down the boardwalk away from me and Walker.

. . .

There wasn't much else to do after they departed. I'd had enough of mourning and remembrance for one day, so we decided to skip the military cemeteries. We got back into our rental car; we'd only leased it for the weekend.

"Can you believe all of that just happened?" I asked Walker, fastening my seat belt as we hit the road.

"I'm at a point in my life where I can believe almost anything," said Walker. And then, more thoughtfully, "After all the time we've clocked together, it makes sense that eventually I'd slip inside one of your delusions."

We drove in silence back to Paris. What more was there to say? There was no ready diagnosis. Folie à deux? Vulcan mind meld? Too much ayahuasca? The only thing that mattered was that Walker had stood up for me.

. . .

Hours later, when we finally arrived at our apartment, I kicked off my shoes and broke out the wine, a nice red Sancerre we'd been saving, some Italian crackers and good French cheese, pears that I'd bought green, which were perfectly on point upon our return, so I sliced them. Dates and pistachios. A box of chocolates, a gift from one of Walker's dancers. I set it all out on mismatched china on our coffee table, put on one of François's piano recordings I knew Walker was fond of, and lit some candles. No need to turn on the lights.

Walker came out of the bedroom in his boxers, slipping a clean T-shirt over his handsome head. He'd washed his face and looked fresher, more boyish. I handed him a glass of wine and he smiled. Old faithful! I felt that smile travel all the way through my eyes and down my spine and shiver into my knees.

That's when we decided to go home, once Walker's show premiered the following month. He'd received an email over the weekend offering him a spot in the Williamstown Theatre Festival, so he'd be going back to something good, and there was hope for bringing the Paris Opera thing to BAM. The few days away had proved curative and provided me with an idea for a crucial scene I'd lacked. I felt for the first time in forever that I could be productive again back in old New York.

After much discussion, I texted our revised plans to dear Kate as we sat on the couch together, Walker and I, as we had for so many evenings over so many years, drinking wine, inhaling music, Walker's arm, heavy and warm, around my shoulder, his scent, musky and male, with a hint of perspiration and a touch of soap, his very being silently sustaining me as I composed.

Marriage is a miracle when it works.

ACKNOWLEDGMENTS

These stories were written over many years in between longer projects. Two of them turned into novels (*The Revisionist* and *P.S.*), one of those was made into a film (*P.S.*). My deepest gratitude to the people who sustained me all this time with their wisdom, generosity, loyalty, editorial gifts, and treasured friendship, including Rick Moody, Catherine Bloomer, Elizabeth Gaffney, the late George Plimpton, the late Lois Rosenthal, Jennifer Egan, Ann Hood, Jill Bialosky, Cheryl Pearl Sucher, Michael Collier, Catherine Barnett, Brenda Wineapple, Lynn & John Pleshette, David Warshofsky, Anne Harrison & Tim Forbes, the folks at *GQ, Tin House, Ploughshares, A Public Space, The Kenyon Review Online,* the crew at The New School and WriteOn (chef's kiss!), and the late much-missed Joanna Laufer, my wonderful editor, Jennifer Barth, and my beloved agent, Sloan Harris. As always, it has been my darling family for whom I am most grateful, Bruce, Zoë, and Isaac Handy. Much love to you all!

A NOTE ABOUT THE AUTHOR

Helen Schulman is the *New York Times* bestselling author of
seven novels, including *Lucky Dogs, Come with Me,* and *This
Beautiful Life*. Schulman has received fellowships from the
Guggenheim Foundation, the New York Foundation for
the Arts, Sundance, Aspen Words, and Columbia University.
She is a professor of writing and Fiction Chair at The New
School and lives in New York City.

A NOTE ON THE TYPE

This book was set in Hoefler Text, a family of fonts designed by Jonathan Hoefler, who was born in 1970. First designed in 1991, Hoefler Text was intended as an advancement on existing desktop computer typography, including as it does an exponentially larger number of glyphs than previous fonts. In form, Hoefler Text looks to the old-style fonts of the seventeenth century, but it is wholly of its time, employing a precision and sophistication only available to the late twentieth century.

Typeset by Scribe
Philadelphia, Pennsylvania

Book design by Pei Loi Koay